Raintree is an imprint of Capstone Global Library Limited, a company
incorporated in England and Wales having its registered office at 7
Pilgrim Street, London, EC4V 6LB – Registered company number:
6695582

www.raintree.co.uk
myorders@raintree.co.uk

British Library Cataloguing in Publication Data
A full catalogue record for this book is available from the British Library.

ISBN: 978-1-4747-0338-3 (paperback)
ISBN: 978-1-4747-0339-0 (eBook PDF)

19 18 17 16 15
10 9 8 7 6 5 4 3 2 1

Designer: Veronica Scott

Every effort b copyright holders of material
reproduced i omissions will be rectified in subsequent
printings if n ce is given to the publisher.

Printed and b

THE EL DORADO MAP

raintree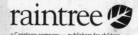
a Capstone company — publishers for children

For Karen and Kendal, who always believed.

CHAPTER 1

THE HOLD UP

As the stagecoach neared the top of the hill, Cody pulled a bandana over his nose and raised his shotgun.

"Stand tall," Pa told him, "and don't do nuthin less I say."

Cody knew the routine, but it always made him nervous. Standing on the dirt at the edge of the road, he listened to the clattering hooves and grinding wheels trudge up the steep, rocky path. He took a deep breath and eased it out as the coach climbed into view.

Pa stepped into the road ahead of the slow moving coach. He grabbed the reins of the nearest lead horse and tugged down hard, forcing the creature's nose to its chest. The horse stopped short, its hooves skidding in the dirt. The other lead veered clumsily into its partner, and the two rear horses jerked sharply against the leather straps of their harnesses.

"Whoa," the driver said, tensing the reins, trying to settle the team. The creatures stomped and snorted.

Pa extended his arm between the front pair of horses and aimed his pistol at the driver. "Howdy," he said.

Silence hung then and the dust settled back to the road. Cody saw the driver glance at the shotgun propped against his seat. The horses shifted nervously. A crow cawed. Cody ran his finger up and down along the curve of his trigger. He reminded himself to breathe.

Finally the driver looked at Pa. "This a hold up?" he said.

Pa sneered. "Ain't that a dumb question?"

From the coach window, a man poked his balding head. "What's going on out there?" he demanded, thick moustache bobbing as he spoke.

"Get yer sweaty head back inside that window!" Pa barked. "Or my boy will blow yer dumb brains all over the side of that coach."

Cody slid the barrel of his gun to the left until it aimed in the man's direction. He could hear voices inside the coach, two women and at least one man besides the bald man. The women's nervous chatter worsened Cody's own nerves. His fingers tingled.

At the edge of Cody's vision, thin birches bent in the breeze. Then a black figure. A man weaving through the trees. Cody's eyes darted to the spot. Trees and shadows swayed. The black figure disappeared in the darkness.

"Pay attention, boy!" Pa stomped his foot. "Now, you, Mr Driver, grab that shotgun and give it here. Slow. And if you do somethin funny, I'll put a bullet in yer face."

The driver reached down and grasped the gun's barrel. He extended it carefully to Pa, who took it and tossed it to the side of the road.

"Now," he said, "get me that strongbox."

The driver climbed down from his seat on top of the coach and stood on the frame between the front wheels. He unbuckled the leather cover, which was strapped across an opening beneath the seat, and pulled the flap aside. "Where do you want it?" he said.

"Throw it down."

The driver tugged a small wooden chest from the compartment and heaved it to the ground. It landed with a heavy thud and rattle.

"Now climb off there and sit yerself against that wheel." Pa pointed with the end of his gun.

Cody glanced into the woods. A crow glided down onto the bough of a birch. The bird's small black eyes scanned the scene, then rested on Cody. It rustled its wings and cawed. The tingle in Cody's fingers crawled up his arms. He heard something stir in the woods.

"Boy, bring them sacks!" Pa hollered. "And the rope."

Cody tugged two burlap sacks and a coil of rope from his belt, and stepped onto the road. "Tie him," Pa said, taking the shotgun from Cody's hands.

Cody crawled beneath the coach and crouched behind the wheel where the driver sat stiffly. Sweat darkened the back of the man's shirt.

"Stick yer arms between them spokes," Pa told the driver.

Cody took a knife from his belt and cut a length of rope. He wrapped it round the man's wrists and pulled it tight, tying one thick knot and then another. He tugged the rope to make sure it was snug and climbed out from beneath the coach.

Pa stood over the strongbox. He angled the shotgun against the corner of the box and pulled the trigger, blowing a fist-sized hole through the thick wood. The women inside the coach yelped at the sound of the shot. Cody heard one of them crying. He didn't think Pa would hurt them, but their bawling made him nervous.

Pa bashed the shotgun's butt into the strongbox to widen the hole. "Get down there and empty it," he said.

Cody crouched to one knee and tipped the heavy

wooden box towards the broken end. Gold coins poured out. He picked one up and inspected it. The word *King* was stamped on each side.

"Quit messin' around." Pa kicked the road, spraying dirt and rocks in Cody's direction.

Cody lifted the box and shook out the remaining coins. Something inside rattled but didn't fall out. He reached in and pulled out a white envelope. It was sealed with a circle of red wax, a bold *K* stamped in the middle. He held it up to Pa.

"I ain't interested in no fool letters, boy. Now bag up them coins."

When Pa glanced at the driver, Cody slipped the envelope into his pocket. Then he shoved the gold coins into the burlap sacks, half in each. He roped them off and tied a long line between the two bags.

"Get them sacks on yer horse," Pa said. He tossed back Cody's shotgun. "Be ready to ride."

Cody hustled to the horses, which were tied to a birch halfway down the back of the hill. He scanned the tree line as he approached, looking for the black figure. The woods were still except when the breeze blew.

He could hear Pa shouting. "Get out here, bald man!"

Cody stepped up to his brown and white paint mare and hung the sacks of gold across its flanks, just behind the saddle. He took two smaller lengths of rope and tied each sack to the bottom of the saddle to keep them from bouncing. He patted the mare's neck.

Pa's pitch dark stallion scraped the dirt with its front hooves.

A crow cawed.

A chill crawled up Cody's arms.

A gunshot echoed.

Cody turned and ran towards the stagecoach. The women were screaming.

"Shut it!" Pa hollered.

Cody came up over the hill. The bald man lay in the dirt at Pa's boots. A red cloud stained his white shirt. The man was dead. Cody knew it. His stomach churned. He had never seen Pa kill a man before.

A pistol emerged from the coach window and blasted with a bright flare. Pa ran towards Cody. He reached back and let off a shot without looking.

Now the driver twisted free from the ropes on his wrists. He rolled away from the coach and scampered on hands and knees towards his shotgun at the side of the road.

Cody aimed his own shotgun at the man and watched him scurry forwards. His finger tensed against the trigger and froze there. He knew Pa would have pulled the shot already, but he couldn't do it. He felt numb except for the tingle of nerves in his arms and chest. He couldn't move. Couldn't breathe.

"Get them horses, boy!" Pa's voice echoed in Cody's ears. He lifted his finger off the trigger and exhaled. He turned and ran.

When he reached the horses, he untied the stallion first and then the mare. He stepped into the stirrup and vaulted into his saddle. Pa reached them and leapt onto the black.

Cody heard hoof beats pounding the road in the distance and closing fast.

Pa glared at him. "Boy, where'd you set them sacks?"

Cody twisted in his saddle and looked down at the mare's flanks. The sacks were gone. His eyes darted to the woods. He spied the black figure moving swiftly in the shadows, a sack of gold in each hand.

The hoof beats were getting close now, shaking the ground.

"Come on, boy," Pa shouted. "Ride!"

Pa launched his stallion down the rocky road and Cody followed.

CHAPTER 2

THE GETAWAY

The hoof beats were so close, Cody could hear the riders calling to the stagecoach. The women responded in shrill voices between sobs. Pa galloped on without looking back, but Cody jerked his mare to a halt. He fought to catch his breath as he scanned the depth of birch and shadows looking for the black figure. He couldn't tell Pa he had lost the gold.

The man's faint outline appeared suddenly, distant and getting smaller. Cody kicked his heels against the mare's sides and it dove into the woods. It cut and zagged through the rows of birch, swift and surefooted. Cody leant low and held tightly to the saddle. Ahead was the black figure and the lost gold. Behind, the thunder and echo of hoof beats.

"Stop!" someone shouted. "Murderer!"

Cody raced through the woods, his eyes trained on the man, a dark shadow crossing lines of thin white birch. He urged the mare on. It tightened its corners, and taut branches slashed at Cody's face. He leant lower and angled the wide brim of his hat to shield himself. Even as he pushed the mare forwards, the black figure grew smaller, less distinct, as if it might vanish altogether.

Hoof beats rumbled into the woods now, and Cody cast a backwards glance. Three riders sped on brown horses through the white trees. An arm extended with a flash and blast. Then a second and a third. Cody spurred the mare and tugged the reins. He angled the horse deeper into the woods, away from the stagecoach and the dead man and the sobbing women. The mare slashed through the thin trees. It raced wildly. The trees blurred. The riders pursued. Gunshots flashed and thundered and echoed. Cody scanned the distance for the black figure. His heart raced. The man was gone. He spurred the mare.

"You can't escape," a rider shouted.

The trees thickened, more spruce now, darker, harder to see. Cody searched, straining his eyes against the fast-moving shadows. He couldn't lose Pa's gold.

He spurred the mare. Tree trunks and brush and dark spaces rushed past. He tugged the reins side to side, driving the horse through the openings. He could feel it straining for speed, its hooves pounding and scraping the dirt, its chest heaving for breath. He drove his spurs in once more.

Suddenly, the dark figure reappeared, a hint of shadow like a fading ghost. Cody yanked the reins hard to turn the mare. Its nose bent low and its rear swung out wildly. It stumbled and rolled. Cody flew from the saddle. Trees and sky blurred. Wind gushed against his face. He landed hard and tumbled, crashed into a cluster of birch saplings and bushes. His heart raced. He heard the mare snort and squeal. He untangled himself from the thorns biting into his skin and wiped a stream of blood from his cheek. He inhaled deeply and climbed to his feet.

The mare staggered. It stumbled forwards and sideways, whinnied and whined. Its front leg hung limply, and it hopped and shifted to keep its weight off the broken limb. Hoof beats pounded as the riders sped closer. Cody's heart pounded.

He felt helpless, watching the mare struggle. He stared at the saddle, the place where he'd hung the sacks of gold, the place where he'd sat only moments ago.

His shotgun was lashed behind it. In his head, he heard Pa's voice telling him to grab the gun – not to go down without a fight. But he couldn't step forward to grasp the weapon.

He heard the riders pull up but continued to watch the mare. Its unbroken front leg buckled and the horse fell to its knees. He heard boots land on the dirt behind him and step forwards quickly. Then a man stood beside the paint mare. He put his stocky frame to the horse's shoulder to help support the damaged creature. He patted its neck and whispered soothing words.

"You'll be all right, girl."

Then he looked at Cody and his face sank with disappointment. "You're just a boy," he said.

Cody stared at the dull brass badge pinned to the man's coat.

"We have to put this horse down," the man said. He drew a pistol from the holster at his belt and held it out to Cody, handle first.

The man's skin was rough and tanned dark, and he stared hard at Cody. "If you've got any ideas," he said, "my deputies are right behind you."

Cody glanced back at the two tall men, still in their saddles, pistols drawn and aimed. "Well?" the man said.

Cody shook his head.

"I see. You can ride a horse to death, but you can't finish the job."

The mare staggered awkwardly on one front leg. It breathed hard, mouth frothing. The man took hold of the horse's reins and eased its nose downwards. He whispered again and put the barrel of his pistol to its forehead. Cody turned and stared at the sky through the treetops. His fingers tingled.

A blast and echo. A heavy thud.

Cody held one hand in the other to stop the shaking.

A small barred window let a sliver of bright spring sunshine into the dim cell. Dust floated and glimmered in the light, and a fly buzzed through the dust. Cody thought about his mother, who he could not remember. The sobs of the women replayed in his mind. Blasts and echoes. Hoof beats. The heavy thud. The cloud of red on the bald man's chest. The paint mare lying in the dirt, still and silent, blood running from its forehead.

Then Pa's bony face filled the window and the cell darkened. "Listen up, boy," he said. "I ain't got long."

Cody stood up from the cracked, wobbly bench where he sat and stepped towards the window.

He had never before felt so relieved to see Pa.

"Did the sheriff get them bags of gold?"

Cody shook his head.

"Good boy," Pa said. "You stashed it when you heard the law."

Cody thought about the black figure running through the woods, a sack of gold clenched in each fist.

"Tell me where it is."

"Ain't you gonna break me out?" Cody said.

"I'm gonna get that gold," Pa said. "Yer just a boy. They ain't gonna hang you."

Cody felt a heavy thud inside his stomach, like the mare dropping to the dirt.

Pa stared with small, dark eyes. "Tell me where you stashed that gold, boy."

"Break me out, Pa. I can show you. I don't want to stay here. It's too dark."

Pa sniggered. He fished in his pocket and drew out a matchstick, which he held up for Cody to see. Then he flipped it through the window onto the planked floor. "You can light yerself a fire," he said, grinning.

Cody stared at the matchstick. He could hear Pa breathing. He could feel him watching. He could hear his boots scraping the dirt. Pa was mean, Cody knew, but he always thought Pa took care of his own. Now he knew he couldn't count on that. Now Cody knew he had to take care of himself.

"You remember where we tied the horses, Pa?"

Pa nodded.

"There's an old spruce with a hole in the trunk where it got struck by lightning. I stashed it in the hole."

Cody wondered what Pa would do when he saw the gold wasn't in the tree.

He stared at the matchstick for a long time before he picked it up. Then he flipped over the bench and pulled the legs off. He broke away some small pieces from the old cracked wood and piled it all against the wall below the window. He took off his shirt and hat and added them to the mound. If Pa wouldn't help, he'd have to break himself out. He struck the match on his boot heel and held the flame to his crumpled shirt.

The fire started slowly. Small flames inched up the shirt sleeve, specks of glowing fabric drifting into the air. A wisp of dark smoke eased its way up and out of the window. Flames crept to his felt hat and smoke hung thinly in the air like fog. Flames crawled up the bench, began to bend and dance. They reached upwards and grabbed at the wall. Smoke flooded the cell and stung Cody's eyes. He coughed. Thick, strong flames engulfed the bench. The old wood crackled and popped.

The smoke thickened. Cody coughed and hacked. He struggled to gain his breath. The cell grew dark with smoke and bright with fire. It happened so fast. Cody knew he'd made a terrible mistake. Flames leapt up the walls and clambered across the ceiling. Cody heard voices shouting. He tried to call to them, but the smoke smothered his words. The nerves in his fingers and arms and chest buzzed. He stared at the wall where he'd expected the opening, but only saw flames. The heat was unbearable. Hair curled and disappeared from Cody's forearms. The flames stood as tall as monsters. Cody dropped to his knees. His whole body stung. Lungs burned. Blinded. He shut his eyes tightly. Heat. Smoke. It happened so fast. Regret. Cody thought of his mother. He would meet her now. He fell to the floor and curled into a ball.

Then coolness engulfed him, soothed his skin. Cody breathed deeply. Crisp winter air. He opened his eyes. White light flooded the cell. Smoke poured away from him. Flames grew smaller and dimmer until they disappeared altogether. A hand reached through the light and gripped Cody's hand. It pulled him up and through the glow.

Cody found himself standing outside of the jail. Before him stood an old man, dressed in black.

Chapter 3

THE OLD MAN

Thick, acrid smoke hung in the air. Boots clattered on dirt as men scurried towards the charred building carrying shovels and buckets of water. The iron bars of the jail cell's window hung at a defeated angle from what remained of the structure's blackened frame. Glowing embers at Cody's boots hissed smoke and heat.

The old man stood before Cody, still gripping his hand. He grinned beneath his neat white beard, green eyes sparkling brightly.

"Thanks," Cody said. He tried to pull his hand away, but the old man held it tightly.

"You ought to scram," the old man said. His lilting voice made Cody think of water.

"What happened to the fire?" Cody said. "Did you do that?"

The old man grinned and shrugged. "See the smokey mustang tied at the trough across the way?" He motioned with his chin. "Nobody around here will miss it."

Cody stared at the man's face, its features small and rounded, skin ruddy and taut. "Why're you helping me?" he said.

The old man finally let go of Cody's hand. "Seems fair," he said.

"You took our gold."

"Your gold?" The old man smiled. He reached up and repositioned his bowler hat. "It's not here."

"I need that gold," Cody said.

"You need to scram." The old man pointed with his thumb, and Cody turned to find the sheriff standing not far away.

The sheriff clenched the brim of his hat in his fist and stared at the burnt rubble. His leathery jaw tightened and he spat. He turned towards Cody and the old man, but his dark eyes seemed to look right through them. "Let's clear this out and see if we can find the boy's body," he barked.

Cody held his breath until the sheriff turned back towards the rubble. Then he looked dumbly at the old man, who shrugged once more.

"He can't see us."

Cody stared at the man. The confusion in him grew, as if there was a question he meant to ask but had forgotten. He felt his mouth open to speak, then close uselessly. He glanced at the men who fought what was left of the fire. Water from their buckets doused the smouldering ashes, which hissed and steamed, and glowed and dimmed. When he looked back, the old man was gone.

Cody strode across the dirt road. Pa always told him to move like he had nothing to hide. He gently untied the mustang and patted its neck. Then he led it away by the reins, keeping the horse between himself and the lawmen.

He turned onto the main road, and moved past a telegraph office and a bank. He stopped and tied the mustang to a post outside a shopfront. A sign above the door read, "General Goods." Cody pulled open the door and a bell jangled.

A portly, bald man stood behind a counter. "Howdy," he said. "Looks like you need a shirt."

Cody stopped, the breath caught in his throat. The shopkeeper looked just like the bald man Pa had killed. He could still picture the blood on the man's white shirt. He swallowed hard and exhaled. "Looks like I do," he said. He forced a smile. "You got one that would fit me?"

The man squinted one eye and appraised Cody. "You're skinny, not too tall. I'd say medium."

"Sounds right," Cody said. "You got any mediums?" He strolled around the small shop. Nails, flour, fabric, tools. He spied some dried beef and some hunting knifes, no guns. He wondered if the lawmen would search the town or head straight out. Either way, he needed some things before he could run.

The back wall was a checkerboard of small pine shelves filled with neatly folded clothes. A row of cowboy hats sat on top of the shelving and another row hung from pegs just below the ceiling. The man took a ladder from behind the counter and propped it against the shelves. "You got money?" he said.

"My pa's comin'." Cody took a small paper bag from a stack next to the dried beef and loaded it full. "He's a banker." He put the bag on the counter beside the register. He drummed his fingers on the counter and watched the shopkeeper. He took a deep breath.

The man climbed the ladder and reached up to the top shelf. He sorted through a stack of shirts and pulled out a blue one with white buttons down the front. He tossed it to Cody. "Try this."

Cody slipped it on, buttoned it up and tucked it in. He looked at the man and smiled. "What do you think?"

"I think you need a hat." The man motioned towards the rows of hats above.

"Suppose I do," Cody said. He pulled a hunting knife and sheath from a wooden box beside a stack of saws. "You got any canteens?"

"In the corner, there," the man said. He tossed Cody a stout grey hat with a wide brim. "Try this."

Cody caught the hat and nestled it on his head. It felt good. "What about that one there," he said, pointing to a round-topped black hat at the end of the row. He grabbed a canteen and a coil of rope hanging nearby. He stepped towards the counter.

The man slowly climbed down the ladder, watching his feet as he went. Cody reached up and muffled the bell above the door in his closed palm. He brought the knife up and cut the string that held it there. He set the bell carefully on the counter. His toes tingled.

The man stepped down from the ladder, lifted it, and

repositioned it at the end of the row. He smiled at Cody, who tipped the grey hat amiably. As the man climbed back up the ladder, Cody gathered his things from the counter and stepped out of the door. He untied the mustang, climbed into the saddle and set his heels into the horse's sides.

They reached the end of the road before Cody heard the shopkeeper holler at him.

Cody rode hard out of town until he came to the hill where the hold-up had gone wrong. He slowed the mustang and scanned the road and the tree line. Thin white birches shifted uneasily in the breeze. But there was no sign of Pa. If he had been there looking for the gold, he was already gone. Cody turned the stallion into the woods.

Then, hoof beats, distant but approaching quickly.

Cody took a deep breath and climbed out of the saddle. He walked the mustang deeper into the trees and stopped behind a thick cluster of bushes. The hoof beats grew louder and slowed. Cody held his breath. He heard voices. He remembered the echoing gunshots. He patted the mustang's shoulder. "Hold steady," he whispered. His fingers tingled. Small, black bugs bit his neck. He thought of the jail cell and Pa's face in the barred window. The matchstick falling to the ground. Boots scraping dirt. He shouldn't have stopped here; he should have kept running.

Cody stayed hidden for a long while after the hoof beats set off and sped up and faded away. He listened to the silence until he felt sure the men had gone. The mustang was quiet and still and he patted the creature's neck to stay calm. Then he led the horse deeper still into the woods. He felt afraid to go towards the road. He found himself looking for a tree with a hole where the gold might be hidden, as if there were truth in the story he had told Pa. He guided the mustang up and down the rows of birch and spruce looking for signs of the gold or the old man's trail. But he knew the old man and the gold were gone. He didn't know what he was trying to do. He kept thinking of the dead man and the old man and Pa. He kept walking the mustang through the woods.

Finally, the sun slid down the curve of the blue sky and the air grew chilly. Birds fluttered in and out of the treetops. Cody stopped. He let the mustang chew on the bushes and tufts of grass. He realized he felt hungry.

They backtracked to a nearby stream and found a clearing. Cody unsaddled the mustang. He crouched down by the water and scooped handfuls into his mouth. The grey stallion leant in beside him and drank.

Cody didn't dare light a fire. He tied the mustang and sat on the ground. He leant back against a fallen tree and chewed a strip of dried beef. He thought about the old man. Cody wondered why he had come back to help him. He wondered how he had put out the fire. The gold was gone, but Cody was alive. He felt thankful despite all the trouble he was in with Pa. He wondered if the old man had a family.

Cody swallowed his last bit of jerky. "Suppose I ought to give you a name," he said to the mustang, "since it's just you and me."

The stallion regarded him and whinnied softly.

"How 'bout Dusty? On account of your colour."

The stallion blew hard through its nostrils and scraped the dirt with its front hoofs.

"Ashes?" he said. "On account of my day."

Again the horse responded with agitation.

Cody thought for a time. "You sure hid good," he said finally. "How about Smoke?"

The grey held silent.

"Okay. Smoke it is. My name's Cody, in case you were wondering."

Cody watched the mustang. It stood very still.

Its ribs moved slightly as it breathed. He thought about the paint mare and the thud when its body hit the ground. He wished they had never held up that coach.

Cody reached into his pocket and pulled out the envelope he had taken from the strongbox. The red wax seal was cracked now. He wondered what the K stood for. He ripped open the flap and pulled out a folded sheet of pale brown animal hide. It was frayed and creased, as if it had been folded and unfolded many times. Cody unfolded it now and held it up to a dim moonbeam that reached down through the treetops.

Drawn in smudged black ink was an outline of the Freelands territories. Cody had seen the image before in newspapers. This map, however, extended beyond the territories, and it was in one of these areas that a gold sun had been drawn. At the top of the map, scrawled in faded black ink were the words, "El Dorado."

Cody laughed. He had heard of El Dorado and its gold, an entire city of gold – rings and necklaces, cups and chairs, streets and buildings. He didn't know what else, but more gold than you could fit in your wagon. It was just a story, but the map excited him.

It led *somewhere*. Maybe not to El Dorado, but to some place worth being marked with a golden sun. Some place Pa would probably never go. Maybe a city of gold. Maybe it didn't matter. Cody sighed and tucked the map back into his pocket.

"Night, Smoke," he said, and closed his eyes to sleep.

Chapter 4

SMOKE

Next morning, the sunlight hung like a sheet of fiery gold above the birch forest. Cody gazed at the sky for a time and decided it would be a good day. He ate some dried beef, filled his canteen and saddled the mustang.

"We got a long walk today, Smoke," he said, climbing into the saddle. "Though I ain't sure where to."

Cody loped up the road on the grey, glad to get away from the woods. He hadn't found the gold, but he decided it didn't matter so much as long as he didn't run into Pa. He wondered where Pa might have gone. He wondered if Pa would look for him.

"You ever been to El Dorado, Smoke?" he said.

The mustang clopped down the rocky dirt road.

"I think I might like to go." He felt certain Pa would

never find his way there – even if it were made of gold.

The morning passed, easy and uneventful. Puffy white clouds drifted through the sky and Cody watched their shadows slide over trees and rolling green meadows. Around lunchtime, a jackrabbit darted across the road, big ears sticking straight up. Cody's stomach growled and he wished he had a gun. He was thinking about how he might catch a rabbit without one when he saw two riders approaching.

Cody leant forward towards the mustang's ear. "Just some fellas, Smoke," he said. "Nothin' to worry about."

The men slouched in their saddles and rode slowly. One was tall with dark hair, the other stout, blond and bearded. The two men stopped just ahead of Cody, blocking the road. Each had a pistol holstered at his waist.

Cody pulled up just in front of the two men. "Howdy," he said, with a slight nod. He steadied his boots in his stirrups.

The tall man pushed some sweaty strands of hair away from his eyes. "We been huntin' an escaped murderer all night," he said. His eyes widened and he glanced to either side. "You pass any dangerous-looking fellers today? Sheriff said he'd probably be on foot, since he ain't got no horse."

Cody patted the grey's neck and smiled. "Got me a horse, right here."

"I reckon he's long gone by now," the tall man said.

But the blond man stared at Cody. He squinted his eyes and scratched his bearded chin. He reached into his pocket and pulled out a crinkled piece of paper. He unfolded it and eyed it carefully.

The tall man leant over to study it, too.

Both men looked from the paper to Cody and back several times.

Cody gripped his reins tightly and leant forwards in his saddle.

"You're him," the blond man said, finally, his rough face screwed up tightly. "You're that kid, ain't you?"

Cody shook his head. "I ain't nobody," he said.

"You're coming with us, kid."

Cody drove his heels into the mustang's sides and bolted between the two men, unsettling their horses. The stallion rode hard, faster than Cody expected. He almost fell out of the saddle and had to tug the reins sharply to keep himself upright. The mustang ignored the jerk on the reins and drove forwards. It galloped off the road and through a meadow of tall grass and flowers.

Cody pulled off his hat and clutched it tightly to keep it from blowing away. Blue and yellow flowers shook and swayed as the stallion cut a wake through the field. Cody watched the colourful clusters streak by like spooked fish in bright green water.

"Yee haw!" he hollered. He couldn't help himself. He had never ridden so fast. He glanced back at the two riders, who had only just reached the meadow. Cody couldn't see if their guns were out, but they were too far behind to bother shooting.

Cody held the reins loosely and didn't put his heels into the horse. The mustang picked its own path and pace. They raced full speed across the meadow, through a stand of pines and up a hill onto a narrow road. When they finally slowed, Cody couldn't even see the riders behind him.

"Smoke, you are the finest horse I ever met," he said. A broad smile stretched across his face.

The mustang breathed heavily.

From around the bend, a fine looking stagecoach emerged. The smallish coach was drawn by four chestnut mares and painted deep red with gold letters on the side that Cody couldn't make out. A skinny black man with a ten-gallon hat guided the horses from his driver's seat. Cody watched him gently work the reins, easing his team around the corner.

The man tipped his hat and smiled as Cody passed.

Cody put his own hat back on and nodded hello. Smoke whinnied.

As he passed the coach window, Cody saw a lady inside. Her eyes were big and brown and her skin was dark like coffee. She smiled widely at Cody as if they were old friends. Cody smiled back and tipped his hat.

As soon as they passed the coach, the mustang stopped.

Cody snapped the reins, but the horse didn't move. He glanced down by the horse's hooves, but nothing blocked the path. No ditches. No snakes. He scanned the road ahead and the open fields to either side for a posse or a wolf. He didn't see any danger. He looked back for the riders. He didn't see them either, but he knew they would catch up soon.

He snapped the reins, but the horse didn't move.

"Smoke!" he said. "What are you doin'?"

The horse snorted and turned and fell in line behind the red coach.

Cody tugged the reins right and then left, and then straight back, but the mustang ignored him. "We gotta go," he said. "Those riders are comin'."

The brown-eyed lady peeked her head out of the coach window. "Looks like you're having some trouble with your horse," she said.

Cody glanced at her but didn't answer.

Smoke snorted loudly.

Cody tugged at the reins again and gave Smoke a sharp heel to the ribs, but the horse continued to follow the coach, unperturbed. Cody could hear the riders now, their hoof beats stomping up the road. He felt his calmness draining away. His head went cloudy. He couldn't think. He tugged and kicked at his horse, but the mustang continued calmly down the road.

"Smoke, we gotta go!"

The riders arrived with guns drawn. They pulled up alongside Cody, and the mustang stopped. One man hovered on either side. They glared and pointed their guns.

"You got any weapons, boy?" the blond man said.

Cody felt foggy. He shook his head.

"He's got a knife on his belt," the tall man said.

"Take it, and grab a hold of his reins." The blond man didn't take his eyes off Cody's. "This time," he said, "you're coming with us."

Cody found himself waiting for the mustang to do something. Rear up and kick the riders. Leap over the coach. Gallop away. Anything.

But when the tall man reached over and grabbed Smoke's reins, the mustang didn't do anything about it.

"I didn't kill nobody," Cody said.

"Kill somebody?" The brown-eyed lady stood in the road now. Her expression was calm and it made Cody feel better. He could see she was going to have a baby by the round belly under her long scarlet dress. The driver came up beside her and she took his arm to steady herself.

"Gentlemen," she said, "would you kindly explain what is going on?"

The riders looked at each other and then back at the lady. The blond man's eyes held their squinty glare, but the tall man's eyes grew wide again.

"This boy's a murderer," the blond man said, the muscles of his thick arms tensing.

"Escaped from the jailhouse," the tall man added excitedly. "Burned it down."

The lady looked into Cody's eyes, and he shook his head.

"That's impossible," she said finally.

"No, ma'am, we saw it. Burned to the ground."

"That may be," she said. "But this boy didn't do it."

The blond man scratched his bearded chin. He looked up at the sky and his face contorted in thought. Then he sighed heavily and looked down at her. "How do you know that, ma'am?"

"Because he works for us." The lady pointed at the door of the coach, which stood open now. A set of gold, script letters on the door read, "Ryder's Saddles and Leather."

The blond man looked at the driver. "Is that so?"

"My wife's no liar."

The man shook his head. "Something seems odd."

"It's not so odd," the lady said. "We have a business and he works for us."

"Then why'd he run?" the tall man said. He tried to look stern, but he looked more like he couldn't remember something.

"Because you chased him, I suppose."

The two men glanced at each other uncomfortably once again.

"Gentlemen, we'd like to continue on, if you don't mind." The lady smiled at them. "We've got an awful lot of work to do back home."

"I guess we was mistaken," the blond man said.

"It's no trouble," she said.

Cody watched the two men ride off. Then he looked at the lady and her husband. The husband held one hand on her back and the other on her elbow.

She rubbed her round belly with her free hand. "You didn't kill nobody, did you, son?"

"No, ma'am," Cody said.

"I didn't think so." She looked at her husband and stared into his eyes for a moment. He gave the slightest nod in reply. "I think you ought to stay with us for a time," she said. "That is, if your horse will cooperate."

The lady and her husband laughed. Cody smiled and patted the grey's neck. He watched the couple climb aboard the coach, heard the man give a low call to his team, and saw the coach pull slowly away.

Without prompting, the mustang followed the coach, and Cody wondered where they were heading.

Chapter 5

A FINE HOME

Cody stood frozen in the doorway. He clutched the brim of his hat tightly. His eyes fell to the floor. This seemed too fine a house to set foot in. A fancy flowered rug lay between a green couch on one side of the room and a pair of matching cushioned chairs on the other. Glass oil lamps stood on small round tables beside each piece of furniture. And small photographic portraits framed in flowery pewter stood on the tables beside the lamps. Most impressively, at the far end of the room, stood a dark wooden piano, its white and black keys shining.

"Come on in, son."

Cody looked at the man, who nodded and smiled. Cody thought to step in, but the woman sprang forwards.

"Not so fast!" she said. "You are dirty as the stable floor. I won't have you wrecking my house."

"Doris, you are going to scare this boy away."

"That is the idea," she said. "Now get him a bucket and a towel and such. Outside."

Cody stood at the well pump and peeled off his clothes.

"Don't you ever bathe, son?"

"Not so much, sir."

"Not so much, indeed." The man clicked his tongue and shook his head. "But you sure did manage to keep that shirt clean." He chortled and tossed Cody a rag and a bar of soap. "Now get to it."

Cody remembered how he had stolen the shirt just one day ago. He was glad the man didn't say anything more about it.

"Drop your clothes in the wash tub when you're done."

"Thank you, Sir."

"No, thank you, because if you'd made that house dirty, we'd have never heard the end of it."

The man set a pair of neatly folded trousers on a rock. "You can put these on and come in the house when you're done."

When Cody was clean and dressed, he headed straight to the stables.

Smoke stood in a wide stall chewing a bushel of hay tied to the door. The mustang looked up when Cody entered, hat clutched in his hand. It scanned Cody's bare chest and his bare feet and his overly long trouser legs, which were each rolled four times to keep them from dragging on the ground. Then it nickered and neighed.

"It ain't funny, Smoke." Cody glared at the horse and scrunched one side of his face in an exaggerated snarl. "You're the one who followed these folks."

Smoke chewed his hay.

"They do seem real nice," Cody went on. "Almost too nice. I'm not sure we can trust em. What do you think?"

Smoke continued to chew the hay.

"Alright, we'll stay." Cody pointed his hat at the grey. "Just be ready to leave when it goes wrong."

Smoke looked up at Cody, straws of hay sticking from its toothy mouth. Cody slammed his hat on, shook his head, turned and stomped out of the barn.

＊ ＊ ＊

"Much better." The woman smiled and nodded at Cody, who stood in the doorway once again. "Come in."

Cody stepped in and stood at the edge of the flowered rug. He could smell spices and a hint of smoke.

"What's your name, son?"

"Cody."

"Welcome, Cody. My name is Doris and this is Jesper. But you can call us Mr and Mrs Ryder." Mrs Ryder held out her hand to Cody, and after a moment, he took it and shook it awkwardly.

When he let go, he said, "I ain't around so many ladies, ma'am."

Mr Ryder held out his hand, and Cody shook it.

"Fine grip," Mr Ryder said. "Now what's that I smell cookin'?"

"Cooked," Mrs Ryder said. "Are you hungry, Cody?"

Cody nodded, and Mrs Ryder smiled broadly. Her lips were full, and just a shade darker and a hint more violet than her brown skin. Cody thought they looked like the petals of a small flower laid upon her face.

In the kitchen, the stove threw off a wave of heat into the hot afternoon air, and the scent of brewing coffee mingled with the spicy meat smells. The room looked as neat as the parlour. A square walnut table and chairs stood in the middle. A blue cloth covered the table, and three plates and a bowl heaped with sliced bread were set on top of it. Cody and Mr Ryder sat down, and Mrs Ryder forked a slice of spiced pork and a heap of corn onto each of their plates. Mr Ryder lifted the bread bowl and held it out to Cody, who took the bowl, grabbed three thick hunks of bread, and piled them beside his corn. When he looked up, Mr Ryder scowled at him. Cody stared back suspiciously and held out the bowl. Mr Ryder snatched it from Cody's hands and set one hunk of bread on his own plate. He handed the bowl to Mrs Ryder, who had just sat down, and shared his look with her. She smiled and winked at him, and Mr Ryder's expression eased.

Cody took this as a good sign and dug into his food. The bread didn't crunch like the bread he usually ate. It felt warm and smelt fresh and tasted like Mrs Ryder had cooked it not just to eat, but to enjoy. Cody stuffed bite after bite into his mouth. And as he gulped down the last piece, he eyed the bread bowl and thought to grab a few more pieces for himself. But before he could do that, his nose remembered the spiced pork that waited steaming on his plate. He took the knife and fork from his untouched napkin and cut the meat in half. He raised one piece, far to big to eat in one bite, to his mouth and tore off a mouthful with his teeth. The pork was nowhere near as tough as the jerky he had stolen from the store. The pork, in fact, was more tender than any meat he had ever eaten. And it tasted so flavoursome that Cody wondered if it was really dinner or if it was some kind of dessert. He stared at the black and red and green flecks of spice on the meat and wondered if they could make the meat he and Pa cooked over campfires taste as good. Cody raised his second slice of meat and tore off a bite, followed by a second and third and fourth bite, which he gulped down hungrily. Cody found himself feeling full and staring at his empty fork. When he looked up, he found Mr and Mrs Ryder staring at him. Mr Ryder looked cross again, but Mrs Ryder wore a smile.

"Enjoying your dinner?" she said.

"Yes, ma'am," Cody said, followed by a small burp.

"Good," she said. "Now, eat your corn."

Cody didn't have much mind to eat vegetables, but he reckoned he ought to oblige after they had shared their table. He looked down at his plate; only the small pile of golden kernels remained. He thought about the gold with King stamped on each side, and how he had lost it to the old man, and how Pa had meant to steal it away himself while Cody sat in jail. Then he looked at his hosts, eating good food and smiling and living in a fine house. He scooped up a forkful of corn and shovelled it into his mouth.

When Cody had cleaned his plate, Mrs Ryder cleared it away and poured three cups of coffee and set out a plate of biscuits. "I meant to have a talk during dinner," she said. "But you were eating so . . . eagerly, I gave you a reprieve until dessert."

Cody took a sip of coffee and looked through the kitchen doorway at the shining piano.

"So would you like to talk about what happened back there on the road?"

Cody set his cup on the table and stared down at the dark liquid.

"Why were those men chasing you?"

Cody shrugged.

"I see." Mrs Ryder reached across the table and placed two fingers beneath Cody's chin. She pushed gently upwards until his eyes locked with hers. "You ought to look at someone when they speak to you."

Cody fought a strong urge to look away and nodded.

"Is there anything you would like to talk about?" she said.

Cody glanced at the piano again. "You have a nice house," he said.

"Thank you. We work hard for it."

"Pa says nobody deserves such nice things."

"Is that what you believe?"

Cody looked down at his coffee and shrugged. He appreciated that the Ryders had helped him and fed him. But he had never had more than wooden chairs and a small stove in a two-room shack. He never had a fancy coach or fancy spices or soft bread. And he certainly never had a shiny piano. He couldn't see how it was fair.

"I'll fix you a bed. And you can work with Jesper in the morning – if you decide to stay."

Cody looked up now, and Mrs Ryder smiled at him, but a little sadly.

"Why did you help me?" he asked. "What if I was the murderer?"

"I just couldn't see a murderer when I looked at you."

"Did you do something bad, son?" Mr Ryder said, leaning forwards.

"I did," Cody said. "But not that."

Mrs Ryder set her brown eyes seriously on Cody. "If you want to talk about it . . ."

"I don't." Cody snatched a biscuit off the plate and put it to his lips without really eating.

"All right," Mr Ryder said, pushing his chair back and standing up. "I think it's time everyone got some sleep."

Chapter 6

WORK

Darkness still clung to the sky when Mr Ryder jostled Cody awake. Cody felt startled for a moment and then calm when he recognized the soft cushions beneath his back. He strained to open his eyes and gave up at a narrow squint, just enough to see a blurry Mr Ryder standing over him.

Mr Ryder shook his head and clicked his tongue. "You sure do sleep soundly," he said.

Cody pulled the covers over his face to keep the light out and heard Mr Ryder chortle.

"Get up, son. Work to do."

Cody rolled off the couch and followed Mr Ryder to the kitchen. They ate eggs and drank coffee, and

Mrs Ryder gave Cody a shirt to wear. Cody didn't say much, but by the end of the meal he could at least open his eyes all the way.

When Cody and Mr Ryder stepped outside, the sun glowed a sliver above the horizon and the sky looked like a dark bowl lifted barely off the earth. Cody shuffled to the well pump where he'd left his boots. They stood beside the washtub with his heap of dirty clothes. He fished through the pile and found his trousers. Then he dug into the pocket and pulled out the map. He unfolded it carefully and studied the gold sun that marked El Dorado. It sat just at the edge of the map, close to where the lines trailed off. He could have sworn it was closer to the middle the last time he had looked. He peered at it curiously for a moment, then folded it and slipped it back into his pocket.

〇〜〇

The barn behind the house might have held pigs or sheep once, but now it was clean and filled with tools and racks and benches. One bench along the back wall held four completed saddles, tanned and smooth. Another held an unfinished saddle frame. Cody could make out a half-carved saddle horn resting beside it.

Mr Ryder hunched over a wooden rack with a brown hide stretched across it. Water dripped from the furry skin onto the clean plank floor. A series of strings ran between the rack and holes at the edge of the sheet, pulling it taut across the frame. Mr Ryder tugged at one of the strings and the hide stretched more tightly. He tied it in place and pressed his palm against the surface. Satisfied it was stretched tightly enough, he clicked his tongue and took a step back to admire his work.

"What are you gonna to do with that?" Cody asked.

"Not me," Mr Ryder said. "You." He pulled a dull blade from his back pocket and handed it to Cody.

Cody took the tool by its smooth handle and looked warily at Mr Ryder. "Me?"

"That's right," Mr Ryder said, grinning. "If you're going to learn to make saddles, this is where you start."

"You're gonna teach me to make saddles?"

"Yep."

Cody stared down at the furry hide stretched across the rack, and a scowl spread over his face. "You just want me to do the dirty work."

"Yep." Mr Ryder chortled and smiled at Cody. "I need you to scrape all the fat and flesh and fur off this hide. No question it's hard work."

"Why don't I help you carve that saddle over there," Cody said, pointing towards the unfinished frame on the bench across the room.

"I understand if you don't want to flesh this hide," Mr Ryder said, snatching the blade from Cody's hand. He turned and began scraping the back of the skin with the dull metal.

Cody felt an uncomfortable heat rise in his chest and cheeks. He felt angry and embarrassed. He could have been convinced to work the hide if Mr Ryder had tried a little harder. He just didn't want to be duped.

"This here is bull hide," Mr Ryder said, scuffing his blade across the skin in jagged strokes. "Stronger than cow hide. But you still have to be careful not to punch the blade through."

Cody watched fat glob and curl and fall away beneath the dull metal. He wondered why Mr Ryder didn't seem angry. Pa would have knocked Cody's head and told him to get to it. But Mr Ryder just kept working. Already, sweat slid down his dark cheeks. Pa didn't even wake up this early in the morning.

"Don't have to scrape too close to the strings," Mr Ryder said, working towards the edge of the sheet. "We'll cut that off anyway."

Cody could do the work, he knew. He wanted to

push Mr Ryder out of the way and take over. But he couldn't ask. He felt his insides burn as he watched Mr Ryder manoeuvre the blade. He wanted to kick the man for not giving him enough of a chance.

"Once this side is done," Mr Ryder said. "You turn the rack and scrape the hair."

Cody wondered if Mr Ryder always said what he was doing as he worked. He certainly didn't want to listen to him now. He turned and walked out of the barn. These people didn't care about him any more than Pa did. And why should they, he supposed, since they didn't even know him.

On the side of the house, Mrs Ryder knelt beside the washtub that held Cody's dirty clothes. The tub bubbled with soapy water and Mrs Ryder worked Cody's trousers up and down a washboard propped inside the tub. Cody approached her cautiously, his boots crunching softly on the dirt. She glanced up and raised her eyebrows, then looked back down to her work.

"Shouldn't you be helping Mr Ryder?" she said.

Cody considered the woman for a moment. He stared at her round belly, which seemed to rest on her lap. "Should you be doing that . . . with the baby?"

He thought he saw her frown.

"This baby is fine," she said, rubbing her belly.

She looked at Cody. "This baby will be acquainted with work."

Cody felt an uncomfortable warmth rising in his cheeks again. "Mr Ryder said I should come and check on you since he was busy."

Mrs Ryder raised her eyebrows again, then nodded. "Aright. Tell him I'm fine, same as always."

Cody watched her sink her long brown fingers into the soapy water. "Will you teach the baby to play the piano?" he said. "When it's older."

"Yes, when the baby's older," Mrs Ryder said. The trousers scratched rhythmically against the washboard as she scrubbed them. "How about you, Cody, would you like to learn?"

Cody slid his hands into his pockets. A tingle of nerves ran through his fingers like just before a robbery. "Yes, ma'am," he said quietly.

"We can do that," she said. "But it's hard work. Can you work?"

Cody nodded. "Yes, ma'am."

"Good," she said, letting the trousers sink into the water. She reached beneath the suds and drew out a sock. "Now get back to the barn and give Mr Ryder a hand."

Mrs Ryder smiled at Cody. The gentleness in her

eyes made Cody feel as if she had cared for him since he was born.

"I never knew my ma," he said.

Mrs Ryder pressed the sock against the washboard but didn't scrub. "She died when I was born, Pa said. So I never knew her."

"And you lived with your pa?"

"I lived with Aunt Tess till I was seven. Then Pa came. Said I could be useful to him."

"Do you miss your aunt?"

"She wasn't really my aunt. She was old, and she slept a lot. I did things for myself, that I remember. Not when I was a little baby, but still small. She's not alive anymore, I don't think. But I reckon I miss her sometimes. She didn't treat me mean." Cody slid a hand from his pocket and rubbed his eye. "I think about my ma mostly. Is that wrong?"

"No, Cody, it's not wrong. It would make your mother happy."

"You're going to make a good mother."

Mrs Ryder smiled. "Thank you, Cody."

Cody went back to the barn where Mr Ryder handed him the blade without a word. Every day for the next two weeks, Cody scraped fat and fur off bull hides and set them to dry. He watched Mr Ryder take the dried skins and wet them and stretch them across the wooden saddle trees he made. And he watched him cut and stitch fine tanned leather and build smooth, sturdy saddles piece by piece.

Mr Ryder showed Cody how to use a rasp to shave and shape a pommel and horn from a raw hunk of poplar. He explained how to build a saddle tree to fit the horse and the rider, though he said it would take Cody years to understand.

Cody started building a saddle straight away. He worked by lantern after dinner, trying to form a perfect curve for his first saddle tree. He felt determined to create a saddle worthy of Smoke.

In truth, the pieces Cody built for his saddle tree looked more like letters of the alphabet than smooth contours to glide between him and his horse. One morning, Mr Ryder inspected a piece of Cody's saddle tree, a cantle that would form the back of the seat. He held it up above his head and squinted his dark eyes. He ran his tongue along the inside of his puffed cheeks and clicked his tongue and shook his head. He looked from Cody to the misshapen wood and back again. Finally, he said, "It takes time."

"You don't like it?" Cody said, his face falling into a steep frown.

"I do like it. You've done some fine work here – hard work." He pressed tongue to cheek again. "But you're still going to have to start over again."

Cody's head dipped, and Mr Ryder patted Cody's neck. "That's just how you learn," he said. "Let's take a ride. I've got a delivery to make."

Chapter 7

THE PONY EXPRESS

Cody helped Mr Ryder load the red coach with half a dozen light-weight saddles and matching saddlebags that notched behind the saddles' narrow, angular horn. Then he followed him inside. Mrs Ryder waited with an old flour sack in her hand. She passed it to Cody. "Apples and bread for the trip."

Mr Ryder continued into the parlour and Cody moved to follow him, but Mrs Ryder stepped into the doorway, blocking his path.

Cody heard Mr Ryder lift the lid of the piano, and craned his neck to see what the man was doing. Mrs Ryder leant her head one way and then the other to block his view. "You're going to Jarrett City to see the bosses," she said, smiling broadly.

"Your bosses?"

"No, we work for ourselves," she said. "The Express bosses."

A sour note sounded from the piano, and Mrs Ryder flinched.

"Don't let them steal your boots," she said.

"Are they robbers?"

"Not really, but yes." Mrs Ryder laughed.

The lid of the piano slammed shut.

"Would you go easy!" she shouted.

Then Cody heard the jangle of coins poured into a sack. It was done quietly, but Cody knew the sound like a pianist knows a familiar tune. When Mr Ryder stepped into the room a moment later, Cody glanced down to confirm the increased heft of his pocket.

They said goodbye to Mrs Ryder and stepped outside through the kitchen door.

"Be back late afternoon," Mr Ryder said.

"Can I bring Smoke?" Cody said. "Haven't ridden him too far lately. I think he could use the exercise."

"Hurry up and get him ready."

Jarrett City looked bigger than Cody expected, considering how far west it stood. From the hilltop where he and Smoke pulled up beside Mr Ryder's coach, he could see neat wooden homes with barns and gardens spread in a wide semicircle against a broad river flowing as far as he could see. Stretches of vivid green farmland painted the settled outskirts, while a single row of stately brick buildings lined the riverbank. Between the buildings and the river stretched a broad dirt road, which was lined with crowds of people on either side. A cloud of dust blew down the middle of the street as if a tiny wind storm was trapped there.

"What's going on?" Cody asked.

Mr Ryder tongued his cheek and shook his head. "No idea, but let's find out." He snapped his reins and started his team towards the city.

"Git on," Cody said, urging Smoke ahead with a tap of his heels. But the mustang scraped its hooves and snorted.

Cody felt himself tense. He scanned the ground, half expecting to find a snake. Then he twisted and peered into the hills behind him, half expecting someone to be there. Alone on the hilltop, Cody remembered the coach robbery and the red stain on the dead man's shirt. He shook the thought from his mind and took a deep breath. He patted the grey's neck. "Everything's fine, Smoke. Just a new place got ya spooked is all. Git on."

But Cody didn't believe his own words. He trusted Smoke's instincts, and he couldn't help thinking that something was wrong. Smoke started after Mr Ryder, and Cody glanced backwards once more. The tall grass swayed lazily along the empty road.

○─○

Cody rode behind Mr Ryder through the outskirts of town. They weaved across the spider-web streets until they entered the far end of the main road. A wooden sign on a stout post marked the start of River Road, which was wide enough for five coaches like Mr Ryder's to drive side-by-side. River Road looked strangely empty except for the dirty cloud moving swiftly towards Cody and Mr Ryder. As the cloud got closer, Cody could make out forms through the dust, skinny boys bent low to the backs of their horses, some swatting at their mounts' hind quarters with a hat or a coil of rope. Calls of "ye haw" and "git up" escaped from the cloud. A thunder of hoof beats drummed the hard packed dirt. A mass of riders and horses – Cody couldn't count how many – skidded to a halt at the River Road sign and turned quickly to line up again. Then a distant gun blasted and the riders shot forwards.

Smoke bolted, too. Cody caught himself in the saddle and leant forwards for balance. The mustang closed the distance between the other horses quickly. Dirt sprayed from their hooves, and Cody squinted to keep it out of his eyes. He clenched the reins tightly. His hat flew off and tumbled down the road behind him. He dug his heels into the stirrups and bounced in rhythm to Smoke's frantic pace.

The mustang's legs extended and dropped and sprang forwards. Its hooves pounded the ground but made contact so briefly they barely seemed to touch. It felt to Cody like running above the road. Smoke stretched its nose forwards and plunged into the dust cloud. The riders urged their horses on, but the closer Smoke got, the slower the other horses seemed to move. Smoke leant and turned and darted between two riders. Slipped past. Dove through the dirty air. Sailed.

Cody and Smoke emerged from the pack and streaked forwards. The dirt and dust that sprayed from the grey's hooves painted a single thin line out of the broad dust cloud. The air in front of them cleared, and Cody saw the townspeople along the street cheering and waving hands and hats. A banner stretched over the road between two tall poles marked the finish line. Cody tugged at Smoke's reins as they passed beneath it, but Smoke kept running. Cody could hear the cheers of the crowd fade as the mustang ran another hundred yards to the end of River Road.

When the grey finally stopped, Cody laughed and patted its neck. "I think you won," he said.

Smoke blew sharply through his nostrils.

Cody wiped the grime from his face with his shirtsleeve. "Let's go find Mr Ryder."

The red coach stood in front of a two-story brick building with a green door and a long rectangular sign that stretched across the entire wall. Gold letters embossed in the green sign read, "Offices of The Pony Express. Fastest Way to Get Your Mail West."

Mr Ryder stood beside the coach with two suited men, one portly and bald, the other slim and bald, both shorter than average. Mr Ryder opened the door of the coach.

"Take a look, Mr Russell, Mr Waddell, finest saddles either side of the Blue River."

"I'm certain they are, Mr Ryder. No need to inspect," said the portly man. He looked keenly at Cody as he approached. "Who's the young fella?"

"That young fella's named Cody," Mr Ryder said. "Friend of the family. And, Cody, this not-so-young fella goes by Mr Russell." Mr Ryder chortled.

Mr Russell smiled, but didn't seem amused. "Saw you race, Cody. Quite impressive. You'd make a fine Express rider." He turned to the skinny man. "He could handle the Blood River run, don't you think, Mr Waddell?"

Mr Waddell nodded.

"Cody's been learning to make saddles," Mr Ryder said.

"That so?" Mr Russell eyed Cody appraisingly.

Cody nodded.

"There's no better saddle-maker this side of . . . well, anywhere," Mr Russell said loudly, as if to be certain everyone heard. He winked at Cody. "Guess you'll be a fine saddler yourself in no time."

Cody looked down at his hands, which still held Smoke's reins. "I'm trying."

"Cody's a fast learner," Mr Ryder said. "And he understands horses. That's half of the trick."

Mr Waddell leant in close to Mr Russell and whispered in his ear. Mr Russell replied with a nod.

"Cody," Mr Russell said, "do you know what we do?"

Cody shook his head. "No, sir."

Mr Russell pointed to the sign on the building. "The Pony Express. We deliver mail between the East and the West – and we do it faster than anyone else. We deliver messages from the president and senators, treaties, business contracts, money, love letters – whatever can't wait." Mr Russell pointed to the racers lining up on the street. "We're always looking for fast riders. And goodness knows, you rode the boots off those other fellas. Why don't you come work for us?"

Cody looked at Mr Ryder who smiled thinly, but said nothing.

Mr Russell thumbed the pockets of his suit vest. "Pay's fantastic for a boy your age."

Cody could picture himself racing along the Blood River, dodging bandits and arrows. Heroic missions. Sleeping under stars. Money in his pockets. Maybe after a few runs he would head down to El Dorado, get his hands on some real gold.

Then he thought of the Ryders. He had lived with

them only a couple weeks, but he already felt at home. He enjoyed the clean clothes and dinner and soft bed. He didn't even mind the chores. He had lived on his own for too long, he supposed – even when he lived with Pa or Aunt Tess. And that never felt all that good. He never felt all that loved.

"I've got a job," Cody said finally, and he saw Mr Ryder's smile grow.

"Can't blame a man for trying," Mr Russell said.

Mr Waddell leant close to his partner and whispered again. Mr Russell nodded and fingered the button of his suit vest. "Would you like to sell the horse then? We need fine horses as much as we need fine riders. We could offer a more-than-fair price."

Smoke nickered, and Cody scratched behind the mustang's ear. "I couldn't do that," he said. "Smoke's a friend of the family." Cody decided he liked that expression.

Mr Russell crinkled his face in displeasure. Then he shrugged and grinned. "Can't blame a man for trying."

Cody and Mr Ryder unloaded the saddles and saddlebags into the Express offices. Mr Russell held open the door and Mr Waddell pointed to a table where they set the saddles.

Mr Russell moved behind a desk and unlocked a drawer, from which he drew a pad of cheques. "You certainly do fine work, Mr Ryder," he said.

Mr Waddle stood over the saddles and bags, inspecting them hawkishly. When he finished, he walked over to Mr Russell, waiting behind the desk, and whispered in his ear. Mr Russell nodded and looked at Mr Ryder seriously. "I'm afraid we've noticed some scratch marks on several of the saddles," he said. "Probably rough handling by your young apprentice. I think perhaps a five per cent discount is in order."

Cody felt a ball of nerves drop into his stomach. He looked at Mr Ryder, who put a hand on his shoulder and winked. "Those saddles are fine," Mr Ryder said. "Inspected them myself." He rolled his tongue in his cheek and clicked his tongue. "I can sell them for full price at the Lewiston market. And you know it, Mr Russell. No discount."

Mr Russell glanced at Mr Waddell, then looked at Mr Ryder. He laughed and shrugged and began writing on his cheque pad. "Can't blame a guy for trying."

Cody and Mr Ryder stopped at the edge of town and ate apples under a shady willow tree. Mr Ryder said that Cody had been a great help and had not damaged those saddles in the least.

"Mr Russell is a good man," he said, "but occasionally he lacks honesty."

"Can he be both?" Cody asked.

"That depends, I suppose. But in Mr Russell's case, I think so."

Cody wasn't sure why, but it made him feel good that Mr Ryder thought so.

At the Ryder's house, Cody stabled Smoke and put out some clean water and fresh hay.

"You like it here, don't you, Smoke?"

The horse chewed a mouthful of hay.

Cody walked to a bin filled with oats and scooped out a pail full. He set it in front of the mustang. "I like it here," he said.

Smoke took a drink. Loose strands of hay fell from his mouth into the water.

"You know, Smoke, I wasn't gonna sell you. Just 'cause that man asked, doesn't mean I was thinkin' on it."

Smoke stuck his mouth in the oat pail.

Cody was watching the horse eat and thinking of turning in for the night when he heard a familiar voice. "Why not sell the horse and steal it back?"

Cody looked up to see Pa's shadowy face framed in the stable window. His dark eyes and crooked smile looked wild and mean as always.

"We gotta talk, boy. I got plans for us."

CHAPTER 8

PA

Cody stared at Pa through the window, a feeling of dread coiling in the pit of his stomach.

"Come on, boy. We gotta talk."

He patted Smoke's neck and took a deep breath. "Be back if I can," he said. Then he walked out of the barn and into the darkening night.

Cody followed Pa silently away from the Ryders' house, through a field of tall grass, and into a tract of hickory and poplar trees. They walked a narrow trail to a pond, where Cody saw Pa's stallion tied to a tree. Its coat was the colour of an empty, moonless night. The horse was strong, Cody decided, but it didn't have Smoke's heart.

A small cook fire, mostly embers now, smouldered in a clearing along the water. A half-full bottle of whisky lay on the ground beside a plate still dirty with fish bones and crumbs. A makeshift fishing pole leant against a nearby tree.

Pa sat down on a rock beside the whisky bottle. "Find a seat, boy."

Though the night was warm, Cody felt a chill in his fingers. He moved close to the fire and lowered himself to the ground. He watched Pa through the thin veil of smoke between them.

Pa reached down and took up the whisky bottle. He uncorked it and took a swig. He pursed his lips and licked them and shook his head. "I 'member when we used to fish, boy. Them was good times. You 'member?"

Cody nodded.

"A hook and a worm and a pole. Simple. Just like life can be if you let it." Pa sipped and peered hard at Cody with his small, dark eyes. "See what I'm gettin' at?"

Cody looked down at the burning embers, and Pa spat.

"Did you think I wouldn't find ya, boy?"

Cody stared at the burnt orange hunks that used to be wood. Some spots glowed sun-bright, others lay dim, coated in dark ash. Cody tried hard to remember fishing with Pa. He felt like he could almost recall, but the memory hung dim, like it was coated in ash.

"Use yer voice, boy. You ain't a little girl."

"I didn't know where you went, Pa. And I was in jail, remember?" Cody kept his eyes down.

"I ain't mad, boy. I just wondered if you knew I'd look for you."

"Reckoned you might," Cody said, glancing up to check how angry Pa looked. But he didn't look especially angry, his eyes looked sad to Cody.

"Sorry 'bout leavin' you in that jail. I just wanted to hide the gold before I sprung ya." Pa looked sideways at Cody. "'Course there weren't no gold. Ain't that so?"

"Pa," Cody said, finally meeting Pa's eyes. "Somebody stole that gold, I swear."

"I don't see how that could be," Pa said. "But I don't reckon you got it either. I'm still thinkin' on that one."

Pa absently corked and uncorked his bottle, which made a small popping sound.

He took another drink. "I ain't here to talk about that gold. I'm here to talk about them folks you took up with." He pointed at Cody, the bottle held tightly in his curled fingers. "First off, they ain't even yer kind. I don't know what yer doin' with them dark folks."

Cody opened his mouth to speak, but Pa cut him off.

"Don't want to hear no answer from you, boy. Wouldn't believe anything you say, anyway."

He took another drink. "First I thought you had a scam goin'. I was proud of ya. That's the truth. But after I watched you a couple days, I knew that weren't the case." Pa shook his head in disappointment, but then smiled broadly.

Cody felt something heavy and tangled unwind in his stomach.

"But it's gonna work out for us anyway," Pa said. "Them dark folks got money. And we're gonna clean 'em out good. You and me. Father and son. Blood. Like it's supposed to be."

Pa stretched forwards and held his bottle over the fire for Cody. "Take a drink," he said. "Make you a man."

Cody took the bottle, put it to his lips and tipped it back slowly. The strong-smelling liquid slipped into his mouth and down his throat. It burned, and Cody choked. His belly felt warm.

Pa laughed. "Give that whisky here, boy."

Cody reached back over the smouldering fire with the bottle, and Pa took it, smiling. Cody felt for a brief moment that this was how fathers and sons should be. He felt like maybe he could be happy with Pa.

"It's like fishin'," Pa said. "You got 'em hooked. Now we just got to pull 'em out the water."

Cody stared at the fishing pole and tried to remember sitting on the bank of a pond catching sunnies with Pa, but the image just wouldn't come to his mind.

"Tell me, boy," Pa said. "What do these folks got that's worth takin'?"

Cody wasn't sure he liked what they were talking about, but he had always done what Pa told him. And Cody had a whole inventory of the Ryder's house in his head because it came natural to him to view things that way. And at the moment, it felt really good to be getting on so well with Pa.

"Pa, you suppose we could go fishin' again one day soon?"

"Sure," Pa said. "Just tell me what's in that house."

Cody felt relaxed and nearly happy. He stared at the fishing pole and felt his lips curl into a smile. He knew what Pa would care about most. "There's a piano . . ." he started to say, but Pa cut him off before he could finish.

"Don't be dumb, boy. You think we're gonna steal a piano?" Pa raised his hand like he meant to hit Cody, but he swatted the air instead.

"No, I . . ." Cody felt the hope drain out of him. And

he suddenly felt a heavy guilt pour into his belly where he'd felt near-happiness just a moment earlier. How could he give up the Ryders so easily? What kind of a person was he?

Cody told Pa about the saddles and tools and the picture frames and the silverware. He had to tell Pa something, but he couldn't tell him about the money in the piano. Not now. It chilled his skin that he had thought to do it.

"That's good," Pa said. "Ain't nobody deserve to have so much fortune, 'specially no dark folks."

Cody nodded and waited for what was coming.

"Tomorrow night," Pa said, "I'll set fire to the barn."

"Pa, they got a business. They travel sometimes."

Pa scowled angrily. "Boy, I ain't gonna wait around for them to set off on business."

"I just thought 'cause the saddles is in the barn."

"Don't think so much, boy. It don't suit you." Pa took a long swig from his whisky bottle, and wiped his mouth with the back of his sleeve. "I don't care 'bout no lousy saddles."

Cody felt like telling Pa that he and Mr Ryder had worked hard on those saddles. That they were worth plenty of money besides. And that you could make beautiful, useful things with those tools if you knew what to do with them, and tried hard enough, and cared enough. But instead, he nodded, and waited for Pa to speak again.

"Listen," Pa said finally, his eyes intense, but less mean. "I need you with me. Since yer ma died givin' birth to you, yer all I got left. We gotta stick together, you and me."

what to do with them, and tried hard enough, and cared

When Cody got back to the house, the Ryders were already asleep. He undressed and curled up on the couch under a thin blanket. He felt confused. He couldn't help but care for Pa, but he cared for the Ryders, too. He wished he didn't have to choose one or the other, but he knew he did. If only Pa hadn't found him. If only he'd never met the Ryders. It would have been easier if he'd stayed in jail. And for a moment, he wished the man in black hadn't saved him from the fire. Then maybe he could be with his mother. He wished she hadn't died bringing him into the world. He felt guilt and sorrow and longing swell up in his belly all at once, and he wondered how it was fair that killing his mother was the first thing he had ever done in his life.

And when Cody closed his eyes to sleep, he saw his

mother, or what he imagined her to look like. She had brown hair and brown eyes, like his own. Her eyes were the opposite of Pa's, big and gentle and kind, and her face was round and her cheeks swelled when she smiled, and her fingers looked delicate and held his hand, and her skin felt soft, and she smelled like lilacs and when she hugged him, he fell into her and felt easy and warm and safe. And he drifted into sleep knowing he would never see her or hold her or smell her hair, but he asked her what he should do, and why she left him with a man like Pa, and if she ever thought of him like he thought of her. And he wished she would answer, but he knew she never would.

CHAPTER 9

THE PIANO

Cody opened his eyes to find Mr Ryder standing over him.

"Out a little late, weren't you, son?"

Cody remembered sitting down by the pond with Pa, and Pa's plan to rob the Ryders. He looked across the room at the piano and felt that tangled knot squirm in his stomach. "I just took a walk is all."

"Well let's take a walk over to the barn now. We've got work to do." Mr Ryder chortled and grinned.

"Sure," said Cody, but he didn't feel much like grinning.

Mr Ryder spent the first hour of the morning showing Cody how to chisel a basic cantle shape from a block of wood. Cody spent the next hour practising with the chisel, and the rest of the morning scraping fat and hair from bull hides. He felt glad to be busy. It helped him forget Pa's plan for a while.

At lunch time, Mrs Ryder brought out a tray of fried chicken and biscuits. She and Mr Ryder and Cody ate together on the grass outside the barn. The sun shone brightly, and Cody felt happy to be sitting with the Ryders. He felt at home sitting on their patch of grass, or working in their barn, or sleeping on their couch.

Halfway through the meal, Mrs Ryder announced, "I'm giving Cody the afternoon off. We're going to have another piano lesson."

Mr Ryder shook his head and ran his tongue beneath his upper lip. He scratched his tightly curled hair. "Do I have a choice?"

Mrs Ryder didn't answer. Instead, she asked Mr Ryder what he would be doing that afternoon.

"Working by myself," he said, and everyone laughed.

When they had all finished their meal, Mrs Ryder collected the plates and headed for the house, and told Cody to come along.

Cody sat on the bench beside Mrs Ryder staring at the white and black keys. She said something, but Cody didn't hear her. He was thinking about the coins hidden inside the piano. Pa would want them all. He would know the Ryders kept money hidden in the house. And he would expect Cody to find it. Cody wondered how he could let Pa take things that the Ryders had earnt with hard work. Pa would say that they lucked into their money and the fine things that came with it, but Cody knew they worked hard because he had worked alongside them.

"Cody," Mrs Ryder said. "Don't you want to play?"

Cody looked up and nodded. He did want to play; he just couldn't concentrate. Across the parlour, he saw the fine rug and lamps and picture frames. Pa would take them all. Anything that seemed fancy and expensive, he would want. He would steal a wagon and bring it to the front door for he and Cody to load with the Ryders' valuables. And later, when they sorted the loot, Pa would pull the photos from the frames and toss them in the fire. That part always made Cody's chest feel heavy, and he knew it would feel twice as bad watching the Ryders' memories burn.

"I did not give you time off to be lazy," Mrs Ryder said.

"Yes, ma'am." Cody shook the thoughts from his mind and looked at her blankly.

Mrs Ryder scowled at Cody, but then she smiled. "Are you all right, son?"

Cody nodded and forced his lips into something like a smile.

"Tell you what," she said. "No scales today. Let's make some music."

Mrs Ryder considered the piano for a moment, then pointed out three white keys and two black ones. "You play those five notes. Experiment. See what sounds good. I'll play the chords."

Cody looked at her quizzically, but Mrs Ryder just laughed. She spread her hands across the keys and pressed down gently. A dense but delicate sound floated through the room. She moved her hands and pressed again. A new sound, and Cody felt the music move. A third shift and a fourth and fifth, and then back to the beginning. Mrs Ryder closed her eyes, and Cody watched her face, dark and smooth and intense. Her fingers bubbled over the keys and the music swelled.

Cody felt the weight on his chest ease. He stared at the five keys. His fingers moved over them, but he could not bring himself to press down. His fingers tingled. All around him, music sailed and swam and darted. And Cody felt his eyes close.

"Go on, son," Mrs Ryder said, her voice musical like an instrument. "Go on."

Cody placed his fingertip on a key. He pressed down just enough to *feel* the key but not move it. It vibrated under his finger as Mrs Ryder played.

"Go on," Mrs Ryder said again, and Cody pressed down. A note rang. He pressed another. He wasn't certain, but he thought they sounded good.

Cody cracked open his eyes and peeked at Mrs Ryder, who looked as caught up in the music as before. He settled his fingers over the five keys, the thumb and pointer of his left hand, the thumb, pointer and ring of his other. He closed his eyes and pressed down. One note, and then another. The sound of the piano reminded him of clouds, dense in the middle, soft and misty at the edges. He played notes back and forth between each hand, staccato bursts, tapping and banging. Then he held down each key for longer sounds. It felt like singing.

Cody knew Mrs Ryder was playing most of the music, but he felt a part of it, like the sound and the feeling was swelling out of him, rising into the air, the pain he felt made tangible and powerful. The pain rose from his chest, floated away like a song. His fingers moved and the song rumbled and his heart beat and the weight lifted. Cody was playing music.

When they stopped, and the last note drifted away, Mrs Ryder looked at Cody with a wide smile, her brown eyes aglow. "That sounded good," she said. "I think you have talent."

Cody smiled, and this time he didn't have to force it. Mrs Ryder's words felt almost as good as the music itself. Mrs Ryder touched Cody's cheek. "Play some more if you like. I'm going out to visit Mr Ryder."

Cody stayed at the piano, but he didn't play. He tried to hold what was left of the lightness. It made him think of the moment when the old man extinguished the jail house fire. The emotion at the surface felt different, but the underlying release felt the same. Freedom.

Cody thought about the old man. The stolen gold. Smoke. The map. He wondered if he would ever follow the map to El Dorado. And then he thought of Pa, and he knew what he had to do to protect the Ryders.

○─○

Cody raced out of the house. He ran into the woods and down to the pond, where he found Pa face down in the dirt, clutching an empty whisky bottle in his hand.

"Pa!" Cody said, crouching down beside his father and shaking his shoulders. "Pa, wake up. I've got something to show you. Wake up."

The wind rattled the broad poplar leaves overhead, and a frog croaked.

Pa stirred, and Cody shook him again. The stink of whisky oozed from Pa's skin and it made Cody angry. He shook him again, harder. "Pa, this is important."

The wind blew hard and then ceased, and silence eased down through the trees.

Pa's eyes shot open and Cody could see the dark anger inside them. Pa bolted upright and grabbed Cody's arm hard so his fingers dug into Cody's biceps. He squeezed and snarled. "What?"

Cody squirmed from the sharp pain in his arm. "Let go, Pa. Please."

Pa spat and threw Cody's arm from his grip. He glared at his son. "What do you want, boy?"

Cody drew back from his father. He tried to get far enough away to escape the whisky smell. His heart raced and his mind felt cloudy. He opened his mouth but no words would come.

"I'm losin' my patience, boy."

Cody stared at Pa. He saw rage rising in his eyes.

Pa's hand curled into a fist. Cody touched the sore spot on his arm.

A frog croaked.

Pa's fist tightened.

The breeze blew and Cody breathed in deeply.

Pa's teeth clenched.

Cody exhaled and shook the cloud from his mind. He reached into his pocket and pulled out the envelope. "I have this map," he said.

"I don't care 'bout no map."

"You'll care about this one," Cody said, pulling it from the envelope and thrusting the half-folded map in Pa's face.

Pa snatched the paper from Cody's hand and unfolded it the rest of the way. He lifted it close to his angular nose and stared at it intently. Then he lowered the paper and glared at Cody. "I can't read like you, school boy, but this looks like a map of the Freelands. I seen them before."

"It is," Cody said, "but the sun. See the gold sun? It marks the way to El Dorado."

"There ain't no gold sun."

"There is, Pa, just look." Cody yanked the map from Pa's hand and held it out between them. He straightened a finger to point at the sun. But his hand froze above the map. The gold marking was gone. El Dorado was gone.

Cody looked up at Pa, whose eyes boiled with rage. "Pa, I swear."

The tree limbs overhead creaked in the wind. Frogs croaked.

Pa drove his fist into the side of Cody's face. Cody heard a dull thud, felt a sharp pain, saw a black flash. He slammed into the hard dirt. He drew his arms up around his head. Closed his eyes. Curled into a ball. His heart pounded, as he waited for the next blow. But it never came.

"Get up, boy." Pa stood over Cody now and jabbed him with his booted toe. He still held the empty whisky bottle in one hand. "Don't ball up like some wounded animal. I ain't gonna kill you."

Cody rolled away from Pa and stuffed the map into his pocket.

"You think I'm stupid, boy?"

Cody shook his head.

"You may not want me to rob them dark friends of yers. But I'm gonna. And yer gonna help me." Pa nodded and glared.

Cody met Pa's stare. He touched the sore spot on his cheek and winced.

Pa threw his whisky bottle at a rock. It burst into sharp, shiny pieces that sprayed out violently then fell gently to the ground.

Cody climbed to his feet and ran through the woods towards the Ryders' house. He looked back, but Pa didn't chase him.

Standing alone in the parlour, Cody felt the tingle of pinpricks in his arms and legs and chest. The tears had started somewhere between the pond and the house, and wouldn't stop. He stared at the piano and cried. He wiped his nose with his shirt sleeve and stepped up to the instrument. He placed his finger on one of the keys but didn't press down. He tried to remember what it felt like to play music, but he couldn't.

He reached forwards and lifted the lid, folding it back on top of the piano. He was surprised to see so many parts and rows of wires. He was not surprised to find the leather sack hanging against the side panel. He reached up and grabbed it by the neck. It was heavier than he expected.

He opened the pouch and found gold and silver coins inside. There was a lot, enough to buy a team of horses, maybe a small plot of land. Cody reached in the pouch and drew out a handful of coins. It would be enough to get him far away from Pa, and get them both away from the Ryders.

In the kitchen, on a table where Mrs Ryder sometimes sat to record saddle orders and payments, Cody found a scrap of paper, along with a pen and ink. He took the pen and dipped it in the dark ink, which clung to the metal tip. He stared at the paper, unsure what to write, but knowing he didn't want to leave without some final word.

Cody wondered what Mrs Ryder would cook for dinner that evening. He wished he could be there to eat it, to sit at the table with them and laugh and talk. He placed his hand on the tabletop and felt it as he had felt the piano key; then he touched the sore spot on his face.

Through the open window, he heard the Ryders approaching. Mrs Ryder sang a familiar tune. Cody looked at the blank paper. He touched the table lightly. He recognized the tune as the same one they had played on the piano earlier. Cody felt the tangled knot unfurl in his stomach. He gripped the pen tightly. The Ryders reached the back steps, and Cody could make out the words Mrs Ryder sang.

Sometimes hearts break . . .

Cody lowered the pen and scratched a single word on the paper.

Sorry.

He raced out the front door as he heard the Ryders enter through the back. He ran to the stables and saddled Smoke. He knew the Ryders would find his note, and see the piano lid open, and find the missing coins – and know he had stolen from them.

Cody led Smoke out of the stable, climbed onto the mustang's back and snapped the reins. "Git on," he said, and Smoke took off towards the road. Cody didn't look back.

CHAPTER 10

THE FUTURE

Mr Russell stood behind a counter, humming and studying a stack of invoices, when Cody stepped through the door. He looked up and appraised the boy seriously, and Cody froze where he stood. Mr Waddell, working at a small desk behind the counter, glanced at Cody suspiciously, then returned to his work.

Mr Russell thumbed the arm holes of his green suit vest, and finally a grand smile spread across his face. "Cody, my boy. Welcome!"

Cody removed his hat and stepped forwards cautiously as if expecting the floor to crack beneath his feet. The click of his boots echoed in the open space as he crossed the room. Mr Russell offered his hand across the counter, and Cody shook it. "Here to sell that fine grey?"

Cody shook his head. "No, sir. Come for that job."

Mr Russell nodded, grinning. "Fantastic news, Cody. We can use you."

Mr Waddell stood and sidled up to Mr Russell. He leant in close and whispered in the plump man's ear.

Mr Russell nodded and then looked at Cody earnestly, pausing for a moment with the thought on his lips before he finally spoke. "Son, I know you're fond of that mustang you've got. But when you ride for us, you're going to have to change horses along the route. Might be easiest to sell us the grey – for safe keeping. We could always sell it back to you at the end of your employment."

Cody thought about it. He wondered if leaving Smoke behind would somehow be best for the horse, a way to free the mustang of Cody's trouble. But he couldn't imagine being alone after what had happened with Pa and the Ryders. Smoke was the only friend he had left. "I couldn't do that," he said. "We'll manage."

Mr Russell nodded and grinned. "Can't blame a man for trying."

He and Mr Waddell led Cody out to the back of the building where they found a long row of stables. Just inside a wide doorway, a large man stood at a table with a map spread on top. He bent over the map, considering it carefully and scratching notes with a dull pencil.

Mr Waddell scuttled over to the man and whispered in his ear. The man glanced at Mr Waddell coolly then straightened his broad body to its six-foot height.

"This is Mr Majors," Mr Russell said. "He runs things on the ground. On the trail, you might say." Mr Russell laughed, but no one joined him.

Mr Majors regarded Cody and extended his hand to shake. He gripped Cody's hand as if he meant to crush it. "We don't usually allow you boys to keep your own horses."

Cody felt himself go tense and looked at Mr Russell, who shrugged apologetically.

"But I understand you have a fine horse."

"That's true, sir," Cody said.

"You'll have to stable it at the first outpost."

Cody took a deep breath. Mr Waddell huffed and sighed and shuffled out of the stables.

Mr Majors narrowed his eyes sternly on Cody. "You cause a lot of trouble?"

Cody took his hat off and looked down at Mr Majors' boots. "No, sir."

"Young man, look up here, so I can see your eyes."

Cody raised his chin until his eyes met Mr Majors'.

"What happened to your face? You get in a fight?"

"Not exactly," Cody said.

"I understand you were staying with the Ryders. Jesper Ryder give you that bruise?"

"No, sir," Cody said. He felt the tangled knot uncoil in his stomach. He wondered how Mr Ryder would react when he found the missing coins.

Mr Majors stared intensely at Cody, and Cody felt the knot squirming inside him like it was trying to get out.

"The Ryders are good people," Mr Majors said.

Cody thought he meant to say more, but Mr Majors only watched him as if he were expecting an answer.

"Yes, sir," Cody said finally. "I just had to move on."

Mr Majors eyed Cody a moment more, then nodded. "All right. Let's get you set up. You leave in an hour."

Mr Majors strapped one of Mr Ryder's saddles to Smoke's back and slung the broad saddlebag, which he called a *mochila*, over the saddle. A stiff leather compartment was sewn into each corner of the bag and secured with a padlock. Cody climbed into the saddle and patted Smoke's neck. He reached down and touched the old Colt six-shooter now holstered at his waist. The gun, his knife and a small water pouch strapped to the saddle accounted for Cody's only supplies.

Mr Majors handed him a folded map. "Up river to the ferry and then west."

"West," Cody said, stuffing the map in his pocket, which still held the crumpled El Dorado map.

Mr Russell shuffled over and peered up at Cody, lifting his chin high. "You are carrying items of great importance, my boy, which we have promised to deliver promptly. Whatever you do," he said, "do not stop."

Cody took a deep breath and looked to Mr Majors, who spat and offered a single nod.

Cody jabbed Smoke with his heels and snapped his reins. "Git on," he said, and the mustang bolted down the road, a plume of dust billowing behind him.

"If someone tries to stop you," Mr Russell hollered, hands cupped around his mouth, "then definitely do not stop!"

Cody and Smoke rode out of town and followed the river north until they reached a ferry where the river narrowed. A shirtless old man sat on a flimsy crate on top of the flat boat. His skin looked dark and leathery and his eyes were grey and unseeing. A white feather hung from a plait in his stringy silver hair.

"You made it," he said, his eyes and face pointed askew of Cody in the direction of the sun.

Cody stared at the old man's strange eyes, which looked like they were covered with a thin layer of fat like the kind Cody scraped from bull hides. "I'm with the Express," he said.

The man nodded. "Come. The weather grows angry."

Cody swung out of his saddle and walked Smoke aboard. He looked up at the cloudless, sun-bright sky and grinned.

The old blind man raised his hand and the mustang nuzzled against it.

"This animal sees things."

Cody patted the grey's neck and surveyed the boat. A stout post with a metal loop fastened at the top stood on either end of the square deck, and a thick, frayed rope ran through the metal loops from one riverbank to the other. He watched the old blind man, who rested his face against Smoke's and whispered to the horse in short, breathy phrases. Clearly the boat needed to be pulled across the river, and Cody couldn't imagine how the frail old man would do it. He stepped forwards and reached to grab the rope, but the man gripped his wrist with surprising strength. Cody glared at him and yanked his arm away.

The old blind man smiled. He ran his hand along the rope as if he were pulling it, but without wrapping his fingers around it. Cody felt the boat shift under his feet as the ferry tugged away from the shore and started across the river. The wind rose and a single raindrop landed on Cody's forearm. The old blind man turned his grey eyes to Cody and smiled again. "Sit," he said.

Cody shook his head.

"Sit and talk."

Cody sighed and sat down cross-legged on the deck, one hand raised, still clutching Smoke's reins.

"Where would he go?" the man said. Thin, dark clouds gathered overhead.

Cody let go of the reins and lowered his arm. "How did you . . . ?"

The old blind man shook his head. "Does not matter." He continued to run his bony hand over the rope, and the boat continued to slide through the water. "Others, I let pull, but you may see the truth. You have already seen such things."

"Magic?"

The old blind man nodded. "Some call it that." He took his hand from the rope and rested it on his knee. The boat slowed to a stop at the mid-point of the river. The sky darkened. Rain began to fall, then quicken, then pour down, hissing like a rattlesnake tail and slashing the water. The knot uncoiled in Cody's stomach and rose into his chest. His fingers and toes buzzed like the rain.

"What's happening?"

The old blind man smiled. He seemed to stare, his grey eyes boring into Cody. "You must listen," he said.

The rain soaked Cody. "Get us across," he said through gritted teeth. "And quit smiling." He touched the butt of his revolver.

"The rain will not hurt us."

"I got a job," Cody said. In his mind, he could see his hand reaching into the pouch of coins. He could see the blur of Pa's balled fist. "I gotta go."

"We will go," the old blind man said, "but first you must listen."

The wind blew the rain sideways. The ferry rose and fell hard on the choppy water. Cody saw the coach on the hill and the dead man, his shirt stained red with blood. He saw himself standing before a fire, dropping photographs into the flames. The taste of whisky on his lips. The paint mare falling. His mother's eyes closing for the last time.

He wiped his brow and blew water off his lips. He gripped his Colt and drew it from the holster. He pointed it at the old blind man and clicked open the hammer with his thumb. "I don't know what yer doing," he said. "But it's over. Get us across."

Black clouds filled the dark sky and dumped rain into the river, which rose and shook with the storm. The man stretched his arm forwards, and Cody's finger tensed against the trigger. His whole body tingled, his teeth clenched. He felt like he could explode through the barrel of his six-shooter and break free of everything. He could pull the trigger and kill the old blind man and his father and his own wasted life all at once. His finger shook. The trigger moved like the piano key, not enough to fire but enough that he could feel it. He looked at the old blind man, his broad, leathery nose, his flat cheeks. Cody could see the dark clouds reflected in his dim eyes. The wind screamed. Cody felt like something was being ripped from his insides. The rain poured down his face.

And then the old blind man's fingers touched Cody's arm, and Cody felt calm. The wind died and the rain stopped, and the clouds disappeared from the sky as if they had been sucked into a great hole. And the boat rested in total silence.

Cody looked at his gun and at the old blind man, who smiled. Cody smiled nervously and uncocked his pistol.

He slowly lowered his arm and slipped the Colt back into its holster.

"You must beware of the Okwaho."

"Oak-wah-ho?" Cody said.

"The wolf tribe. They were the great tribe of the mountain. Feared. But respected. Now they are barely men." A drop of rainwater slithered down the old man's face.

"What happened?" Cody said.

"They wanted to own the land. Like the white men. They came down from the mountains to push the other tribes from their hunting grounds. They made deals with the dark spirits to make weapons of our brother wolves."

Cody stared at the man's strange, discoloured eyes.

"The rage of the dark spirits sickened both the wolves and the men. Now the men are more like beasts. And the wolves are lost to themselves."

Cody felt a sadness, as if he had lost something himself.

"They will come for you."

"The wolf tribe . . . for me?"

"When they could not take the land, they made deals with the white men. Now they serve them. You carry something of great importance to the white men."

Cody glanced at the *mochila* draped over his saddle.

He could pick the locks, he supposed, but he wasn't sure he wanted to know what was inside.

"What should I do?" he asked, still staring at the saddlebags.

"I can not tell you, but I have told this horse what will happen. When the time comes, he may know what to do."

Cody looked at Smoke and then at the old blind man, who was again pulling the boat across the water.

"How do you know these things?" Cody said.

"I do not know. I see. They are not the same." He smiled and began chanting softly.

Cody watched the cloudless sky as the ferry moved across the river. He touched the water-logged brim of his hat, which hung limply towards his eyes. His jeans clung to his legs. He thought of Mrs Ryder washing his trousers in the washtub in the yard and of wearing Mr Ryder's trousers that were four cuffs too long.

"They will forgive, if you ask," the old blind man said.

Cody's eyes snapped towards him. "I don't know what yer talking about."

"It will rain again tonight." The boat bumped against the riverbank.

Chapter 11

STORM RIDERS

Cody and Smoke raced down a broad trail beneath a bright half moon. They climbed out of the river valley into the hills, which rose and rolled like waves. The world looked grey and smoky under the moonlight. The cicadas droned like agitated ghosts, and bats flew from stands of walnut trees along the trail to suck down misquotes and moths. The breeze carried the smell of wet grass.

Cody balanced in the saddle and scanned the horizon for Okwaho. He thought about the last time he had ridden this hard, escaping the deputies and meeting the Ryders. And before that, running the paint mare to death. He listened to Smoke's breath and the rhythm of its hooves on the dirt. The mustang could keep this pace for hours, he decided, though he expected to reach the outpost in another hour.

The rain came suddenly, pouring from the sky like an over-turned bucket. Fat drops plunged through the night and exploded against Cody's face and clothes. Small gullies along the trail gurgled with streaming water, and puddles formed over the trail. Smoke bent his nose forwards trying to deflect the rain. Cody simply held tight to the reins. He felt no surprise at the sudden storm, as he was expecting it. He believed the old blind man on the ferry. And he watched for the wolf tribe.

If the Okwaho came, Cody was uncertain what he would do. Smoke already carried them at a hurried pace. He hoped the mustang's speed would be enough to protect them. The rainwater running through his eyes blurred Cody's vision, and he worried that by the time he spotted the Okwaho it would be too late to avoid them.

The night grew darker as drifting clouds veiled the moon. Looking through the long, thick streaks of rain and shadow was like looking at the world through scratched and grimy window glass. Unable to see beyond the trail, Cody felt closed in and alone. He hoped the mustang's vision was stronger than his own. He had to trust that Smoke could find the way safely.

Veins of lightning sliced into the darkness and lit the dark hills with great bursts of light. Bolts of thunder shook the ground and Cody's insides. He felt the familiar tingle, his nerves shaken loose and uncoiling the fear within him. He tried to remind himself that the rain and darkness made the world seem more grim than it truly was, but he couldn't help wondering if he had made a mistake by joining the Express. He was running from the only people he knew, the only people who cared for him.

Lost in his thoughts and fears, Cody was barely looking for the Okwaho when a lightning flash revealed two shadowed figures, a man and a large animal, on top of a distant northern hill. The animal looked too large to be a wolf, but Cody could not imagine what else it might be. He pulled hard on Smoke's reins and the horse skidded to a stop in the mud. He stared up at the dark hilltop waiting for the storm to light the sky once more. But when lightning finally flashed again, the figures were gone. Cody knew they searched for him as the old blind man foretold. He put his heels to Smoke, who leapt into the punishing rain.

The outpost stood nearly on top of the trail. A wooden sign marked "Pony Express" hung beside the door of the small, plank-walled shack. A stable large enough for two or three horses stood behind the main structure. A skinny, hatless man stood outside the stable with a white horse. He wiped rain from his eyes, patted the animal's nose and then waved to Cody.

"Let's go!" he shouted, as Smoke skidded off the trail and stopped at the man's feet. "Get off that horse. You're late."

The man waved an arm impatiently. "Come on, come on, come on."

Cody slid out of his saddle, and the man darted over and tore the *mochila* off it. He slammed it down on the white mustang's identical saddle and checked the cinch to make sure it held tight. "Quit wasting time, boy!"

Cody untied the water skin from the back of his own saddle and hung it over his shoulder. The man motioned again for Cody to hurry.

Cody looked at Smoke. He thought he'd have a little longer to explain to the mustang why he was leaving it here. After what happened to the paint mare, he could not risk running Smoke another leg of the route.

"Time to go, boy."

Cody touched Smoke's neck. "I'll be back tomorrow." It was all he could think to say.

Smoke whinnied and slapped his hooves down on the mud.

"Sorry," Cody said, "I gotta do this."

Smoke snorted and swung his head in agitation.

"Stay with this man till I get back," Cody said, climbing onto the white horse. He looked down at the man, who handed him the reins. "What's her name?" he said.

"This mare ain't got no name," the man replied. "We don't name 'em, we just ride 'em."

"Take good care of my horse," Cody said as he put his heels into the white mare.

The fleet white mare carried Cody down the trail into a forest of pine and spruce. The path darkened with shadow beneath the tall trees, but the rain that reached them through the forest canopy fell more softly. The white mare seemed to know the way, and Cody let it lead. It ran fast and sure-footed, but Cody felt strange riding a horse other than Smoke. He felt guilty for leaving his horse behind with the impatient stableman. And he felt guilty for abandoning the Ryders. He thought about the saddles he had ridden in tonight, still comfortable after thirty fast miles. Mr Ryder made those saddles, and he would have taught Cody to make saddles just like them. Cody could have learned a useful trade, a skill that people would have paid him to perform, something that he wouldn't have to steal, something that no one could take from him. It pained him to think he had missed his opportunity.

Cody even felt guilty for running from Pa again. Pa could say mean things, or leave him in jail, or hit him, but Cody always waited for those times when Pa would say *good job*, or he would sleep and Cody would sit beside him and look at the stars. Those times, which usually started with a good haul and a bottle of whisky and a camp fire, Cody would stare up at the bright specks in the sky and think about his mother. He knew she would have loved him more than Pa did and paid more attention to him than Aunt Tess did. He knew she would have, because that's what mothers did.

Now he thought about Mrs Ryder. She would make a fine mother to the baby in her belly. It seemed like she always knew what to say, or not say, to make Cody feel better.

Sometimes, she even let him stay sad or grumpy. She once told him that those feelings were important, too. And she let him play music. Before that, Cody didn't know a boy could let his feelings escape that way. He thought he could only bottle them up and wait for them to pass. He felt good now just knowing that wasn't true.

When they emerged from the forest, the rain pounced on them once more. The moon hung lower and clouds still crowded the sky. Rainwater flowed over the trail like a shallow stream. Wind howled loudly and the boom of thunder echoed through the night. Lightning flashed and Cody spotted a distant river in the valley below.

Another flash and he saw the dark, square shape of the outpost.

Flash. Two figures in the hills.

Darkness. The figures disappeared.

Cody scanned the hills.

Flash. They reappeared.

Boom. Gone before the thunder crack.

Cody turned in the saddle, craned his neck trying to find them. The white mare raced through the storm. Water poured over them. Wind pushed against them.

Flash. A searing streak in the sky. Cody saw them clearly. No Okwaho. A man standing beside a buffalo.

Cody pinned his heels to the mare's flanks; they sped over the watery trail, down into the valley towards the outpost. Cody didn't dare to look back again.

Chapter 12

FOLLOWED

Cody leapt out of his saddle and stumbled into a tall, weed-thin boy with a floppy brimmed hat. His momentum carried his face close to the boy's bony, brown face and he looked wildly into his dark eyes. "Someone's following me," he blurted. He felt his heart pounding like the white mare's hooves.

The skinny boy's eyes widened and his long jaw sprang open as if he meant to holler, but no sound came out. His head wagged and his mouth twitched as if he were caught at the beginning of some unspeakable word. Rainwater poured from the brim of his hat.

"Now settle down, riders," a man said, gripping Cody's shoulder.

Cody spun and found a fat, bearded man standing

there. The man wore a long coat that dragged behind him like a king's robe, and his bulbous nose flared above a smile that seemed too broad for the occasion. He laughed and slapped Cody's arm. "Who would be out in this weather? Certainly no man with the wits to follow a swift rider like yourself."

Cody felt his own words stifled in his throat. Something about the man made him unsure what to say. He could feel his own jaw twitching without a sound.

The man scratched his blond beard with stubby fingers. He spat and shook his head, grinning. "You boys sure have got imagination." He looked up at the rain, then turned his face seriously towards Cody's. "Not that I'm criticizing. I'd see ghosts in the shadows, too, if I was trekking in this weather. That's why I never became an Express rider myself."

Cody glanced at the skinny boy, who shrugged. "*Loco*," he whispered.

The man spat and slapped his stubby mitt against Cody's back. "Someone following you in this weather. A crazy man, maybe. But it seems all the crazy men are standing right here." He looked from one boy to the other. "We're talking about ghosts. What's crazier than that?" He grinned broadly, his mouth ready to burst with laughter.

But Cody felt no urge to laugh with the man. He scowled and wiped the rainwater from his brow. "A man and a buffalo," he said. "I seen 'em twice." He held up two fingers to emphasize the point. "They followed me."

Now the fat man's grin withered. His blue eyes glanced at the skinny boy, and then he scanned the hills. Finally, he looked at Cody and shook his head in a fast, fluttering motion. "No one's ever seen the Tatanka this far east."

Cody looked at the skinny boy, whose face had paled. He leant towards Cody and whispered, "Buffalo riders."

"Heck," the fat man said, grabbing his beard, still shaking his head, "I'm not sure anyone's ever really seen them. They're legend. A scary story. Something you imagine on a dark, rainy night."

"Where I come from, they know the Tatanka," said the skinny boy. "They are real. And they are fierce. My people do not cross them."

The fat man grabbed Cody by the shoulders, his eyes suddenly wide and wild. He dug his fingers into Cody's bones and shook him hard, jerking his neck violently. Cody's hat tumbled off and landed in the mud. "What do they want with you, rider?"

Cody threw his arms between the fat man's and

bashed his forearms, breaking the man's grip. He leapt back and touched a hand to his pistol. The fat man did the same.

Cody's eyes narrowed. He listened to the fat man's quick breaths, which crossed rhythm with the pounding rain. He watched the man's cheeks twitch, lips rise and eyes squinch in one nervous motion. Drops of rain rolled down the man's furrowed face. Lightning flashed and thunder boomed like a gun blast. A distant bird's caw mingled with the howling wind. Cody felt the Colt's smooth walnut handle against his palm.

Now, the skinny boy stepped forwards, though not so close as to get between them. He smiled brightly as if they were all sharing a joke. "This would be a mistake," he said. "You are so close together, you would surely both die."

"Mind your business, Eduardo," the fat man snapped. "This young rider brought serious trouble to us, and I want to know why."

Cody's wet fingers tingled. Eduardo laughed nervously. The dark shadow of a bird fluttered by.

"You knew they were following you, and you brought them here anyway." The fat man spat water off his lips. "Are you that foolhardy?"

The buzzing crawled up Cody's arms as the cold

rainwater washed down them. "I just saw they was followin me back on that hill," he said. "I didn't try to bring 'em here."

"*Accidente*," Eduardo said, raising his palms.

"Besides," Cody said. "I didn't know they was buffalo riders. I thought they was Okwaho."

"Okwaho?" the fat man brayed, raising his gun halfway out of its holster. "You've got the Okwaho after you, too? I ought to kill you now. Maybe they'll let us be." He wiped water from his eyes with the back of his sleeve.

"I ain't seen the Okwaho," Cody said. "I just thought they might come."

"What could you have possibly done to bring on this much trouble?"

Cody looked at the skinny boy, who had dropped his long arms to his sides and was staring at something out in the rain. Cody followed his gaze to the white mare and the *mochila* slung across its back.

"The saddlebags," Cody said. "They must want what's in them bags."

The fat man gave a single nod, snorted and spat. He turned and scanned the dark, rain-soaked hills. "Ok," he said, setting his pistol back into its holster. "That's a start."

Cody let his hand slide off the Colt's handle. "You got a key to them bags?"

"We can't open those. Only at the end of the route." The fat man wiped his palm down his face, starting high on his forehead and ending with a tug of his beard. He looked sideways at the skinny boy, his face screwed down tight.

"Eduardo," he said, "you've got to get those bags out of here. You've got to go now, before they decide to come down here and take them."

Eduardo held his palms forward and pushed them outwards as if he were shoving the task away. His mouth swung open and twitched silently. He shook his head and finally got out a single *no*. Then he smiled and shook his head some more. He looked at Cody. "No," he said again.

The fat man's face grew red as one cheek squinched up again. He breathed hard and quick and turned towards Eduardo. "You're afraid," he said. "I know, and I don't blame you. But you've got to get those bags out of here. And you've got to do it now." He lifted his revolver from its holster and extended his arm towards the boy, cocking the hammer as he did so. The dark bird cawed.

Then lightning flashed and Eduardo's arm shot out, gun in hand, hammer cocked. He moved so fast that Cody felt unsure he'd seen it happen.

"Let's put these guns away and talk," Eduardo said.

"You first," the man said. He blinked repeatedly and wiped water from his eyes with his hand.

Eduardo smiled broadly. "You are *loco*," he said.

"*Si*," said the fat man. He spat.

"I cannot go," said Eduardo. "The Tatanka can have the *mochila*."

Cody slipped the Colt from its holster.

"You can go or you can die here," the fat man said, his pudgy finger tense against the trigger.

Cody extended his arm and placed the Colt's grey barrel against the fat man's matted blond hair.

The fat man glanced sideways at Cody without turning away from Eduardo. "What are you doing, rider?"

Cody didn't answer. He wasn't sure. He didn't think he could actually pull the trigger, but he didn't want the fat man to kill Eduardo. And Pa had taught him that a man with a gun to his head would always change his mind. It was the kind of thing Pa understood, and Cody trusted that it was true. He held his breath and waited to see the fat man's reaction.

The man looked between the boys several times, seeming to consider his options, though Cody could not guess what they might be. Finally, he shrugged. "Eduardo, you going to shoot me if I lower this gun?"

"I don't want to shoot no one," Eduardo said. He glanced at Cody and smiled. "You, my new friend, are *loco* as well."

The fat man uncocked his trigger and brought the gun to his side.

"Put it on the ground," Cody said. His palm buzzed against the Colt's worn handle. "Real slow."

The fat man squinched his cheeks and crouched slowly to the ground. Cody followed his movement with his revolver. The man set his gun on the wet ground, opened his pudgy hand, and lifted it away from the weapon. He stood slowly, shook his head, and spat.

Eduardo bent forwards and grabbed the gun from the mud. He turned the pistol in his hands and examined it. "Not bad," he said. He looked at Cody and a broad smile stretched across his bony face.

"What now?" the fat man said.

Cody and Eduardo exchanged glances.

A whizzing noise cut through the wind and a twirling hatchet slammed into the back of the fat man's blond head. He fell forwards and landed with a dull thud and a small splash. His fat face sank into the mud up to his ears, and dark blood spread from the opening where the hatchet had lodged in his skull.

Eduardo's eyes popped wide. Cody gasped. The dark bird cawed loudly. A wild chorus of screams and howls erupted in the hills.

Chapter 13

GUNFIGHT

The Okwaho clambered over the hills like wild beasts, half-hunched, mouths agape, teeth bared, dirty and barely clothed. They swung tomahawks and wailed as they lurched forwards. Dark, sharp-eyed wolves ran beside them, muzzles stretched forwards, backs low, hair matted with rain. A rumbling growl seethed from the pack as they rushed towards Cody and Eduardo.

Cody looked at the fat man, face down in the mud.

"He's dead," Eduardo yelled. "Fight!" He raised his long arm smoothly, cocking the hammer in the same motion. He paused long enough to inhale before squeezing the trigger. The hammer snapped down, igniting the gunpowder and propelling the small lead bullet out through the moonlit night between drops of rain and into the dark, bare chest of a charging Okwaho. His war cry died in a sharp gasp as he dropped to his knees and toppled forwards into the mud.

Cody drew his Colt. A low shadow rushed towards him, a black wolf. Its yellow eyes narrowed in the darkness. Teeth clenched jaggedly. Throat droned a deep snarl. Cody held his breath, hand shaking as he raised his weapon. The wolf bounded towards him. In quick succession, Cody aimed, drew back the hammer, and pulled the trigger. His arm jerked. An orange flash and thunder. Smoke. Still the yellow eyes speeding towards him. A rising growl. Sharp teeth set wide to strike. Then a second gun blast. Blood and black fur. Cody watched the wolf tumble across the ground and come to rest at his feet. He hadn't fired a second shot.

"Don't waste bullets," Eduardo shouted. "If you can help it." He grinned, and Cody took a breath. Eduardo turned and fired once and again. One wolf and one Okwaho dropped.

Cody pointed his revolver at a charging wolf. He pulled the trigger and the creature crashed to the ground, blood and mud spattering where it landed.

The stone blade of a spinning tomahawk whizzed past Eduardo's head.

Cody turned and spied an Okwaho bounding towards

the boy. He seemed to hang in the air, his long, sinewy legs bent sharply and drawn nearly to his chest. As he landed, they drove downward, slamming his bare feet into the mud. Long stringy hair and strands of wolf pelt swung wildly around his head. His amber eyes glinted in the moonlight. Nose flared. Jaws sprang wide as if he meant to tear Eduardo's flesh with his teeth. He reached his arm back, fist clenching the handle of a tomahawk. The stone blade hovered behind his head. A war cry erupted from his mouth. Spit and rain sprayed from his lips. The muscles of his arm stretched and tightened. He inhaled sharply.

Cody found his own arm stretched forwards. His thumb touched the cold metal hammer of his Colt and drew it back. The revolver moved with his eyes, followed the path of the dark-skinned warrior. His hands and forearms tingled. His heart pounded in his ears. His finger tensed against the smooth trigger. When the warrior's arm started forwards, Cody pulled the trigger.

Though the gun cracked and echoed thunderously, Cody heard nothing. The world went silent as the bullet plunged into the chest of the Okwaho warrior. A splash of crimson blood burst into the night and fell to the ground with the rain. The tomahawk lurched into the dim sky and tumbled to the ground. The warrior turned his head towards Cody, his bright eyes wide, face tightened in pain and surprise. He clenched his teeth and stepped forwards.

Cody watched as the Okwaho's foot slapped down in the mud and slipped forwards. His leg extended awkwardly and he toppled over. Anger flashed in his eyes and he drew a shallow breath and dug his fingers into the mud. He clawed towards Cody, face down in the rain-soaked earth, then convulsed, then became still. Cody pointed his gun at the warrior, even after he stopped moving.

Eduardo grabbed Cody's arm and tugged him forwards. The Okwaho scurried all around them, calling to each other in a snarling, guttural language. Eduardo pushed Cody towards the white mare and leapt on his chestnut, firing off one shot as he leapt and another as he landed. Cody ran towards the mare. From behind, a strong hand gripped his wrist. Cody swung his free arm backwards. The steel casing of his Colt connected with his attacker's nose and the hand loosed its grip. When Cody reached the mare, he threw his boot into the stirrup and swung into the saddle.

"Git up," Cody commanded, spurring the horse forwards. He spotted Eduardo ahead and steered the mare towards him.

Heavy streaks of rain etched the steely moonlit sky. The Okwaho and their wolves appeared as shadows and howled like night spirits set wild. The wolves ran underfoot of the white mare and snapped at its legs. The horse stumbled and slid in the mud and commotion but held its footing. Cody aimed his pistol down and fired. A wolf yelped and tumbled away behind them. Then Cody felt a sharp pain in his foot. One of the beasts had bitten through his boot and plunged its fangs into his flesh. It half-ran, half-stumbled beside the mare, thrashing its neck from side to side, twisting and tearing at Cody's limb. Cody kicked and yanked, trying to free his foot from its crushing grip. But the wolf clung there, its weight pulling both horse and rider off balance. More than once the mare staggered and nearly toppled over, and more than once Cody nearly fell from the saddle.

The Okwaho ran far behind now, but the wolves still pressed. Cody kicked and let off another shot. He missed the wolf at his boot, but nicked another, which yipped and rolled away. He pulled the trigger again. The hammer snapped harmlessly into the empty chamber. Cody holstered the Colt and gripped his reins tightly. He spotted a large outcropping of rocks at the base of the hills and steered the mare towards it, hoping he could bash the wolf against the sharp edges. Fearing he would take down the mare too, he strained to push his leg outwards and force the beast away from the horse. Then, a moment before impact, a distant shot blasted and the slightest dull impact sounded at Cody's foot. The wolf unclenched its jaws and stumbled forwards. Its body jerked and dropped to the ground, sliding across the wet grass and slamming into the rocks. The silhouette of Eduardo's lanky frame stood halfway up the hillside, the long barrel of a rifle extending from his hands.

Cody shook his foot and grimaced at the pain. "Git up!" he called to the mare.

The horse continued up the rise, the remaining wolves left behind, the Okwaho even further behind. Cody felt a smile rise to his lips. He couldn't wait to reach Eduardo and thank the skinny rider. He never saw the wolf that leapt from behind the rocks until it collided with his chest. He toppled out of his saddle and crashed to the soggy ground. He half-slid, half-tumbled down the hill, cracking his knee on a large rock along the way. His body flopped one final time with a muddy splash and he found himself flat on his back, an angry grey wolf standing over him.

The wolf growled, and the skin around its mouth tightened to reveal deadly sharp teeth. Ears flattened aggressively against its head, it leant low towards Cody so their noses almost touched. Cody felt the beast's hot breath on his face, the smell of rotted meat. He could see in its eyes, grey with black centres like deep holes, that the wolf wanted to tear the flesh from his bones.

Cody pressed his head back against the spongy wet earth to create some space between them. He squirmed and dug his heels into the mud, trying to inch away on his back. But when he moved, the wolf snarled and edged forwards. Cody froze.

An Okwaho clambered from behind the rocks to stand beside the wolf. He looked down at Cody and pointed at the boy with his tomahawk. He hollered in a language Cody didn't understand and shook the tomahawk above his head. He looked back at the field and hollered, then looked at Cody and laughed.

The Okwaho wore a buckskin breechcloth and moccasins. A necklace, tight to his throat, displayed a row of wolf fangs. Plaited strands of grey fur clung to his wild black hair. Two streaks of crimson war paint streaked one cheek. He raised the tomahawk above his head and jerked it forwards towards Cody, who drew up his arms to block the blow. But the warrior stopped mid-strike. He pointed at Cody with the weapon and laughed.

Cody shuddered. He thought about the Okwaho he had killed only moments before and half-wished that this cruel warrior would strike him down now. That tangled knot uncoiled in his stomach and snaked through his body, buzzing every nerve from his chest to the tips of his toes. His lungs felt tight and his head ached violently. He began to shiver in the cold. His heart raced. Blood pounded in his ears. He felt dizzy.

The wolf snapped its jaws and growled and howled. The Okwaho hollered and laughed.

Cody turned on his side and wretched and threw up. He wiped his mouth with the back of his hand. The Okwaho laughed again.

With his head resting in the mud, Cody heard a dull pounding and felt the earth begin to shake. A distant rumble grew and rolled towards them from beyond the hills. The Okwaho dropped to his knees and set his ear to the ground. The wolf raised its muzzle and sniffed the air. It turned a tight circle and then faced the hill and howled. The clamour drew nearer and rose to a thunderous tumult. The Okwaho stood. He closed his eyes and touched the fangs at his neck. Then he raised his tomahawk, loosed a terrible war cry, and raced up the hill, wolf at his side.

CHAPTER 14

RIDERS

Cody climbed to his feet and peered up the hillside. The Okwaho, a shadow in darkness and rain, rose up the muddy slope like a wild spirit. The wolf trailed him like a hungry grey ghost. Moonlight spilled over the hills, pouring dull grey light through the slats of rain. A dead, leafless tree silhouetted on the hilltop shook and blurred with the growing rumble.

Four buffalo appeared as voids in the dim light, cresting the valley's peak. Moonlight sprayed from behind them into the night. For an instant, they seemed to hang at the edge of the sky, silent and weightless, the moon frozen behind them. Then they crashed forwards, at once propelled by their powerful legs and pulled by their substantial mass. The wet earth exploded and splattered where their hooves landed. And as their bodies angled down the steep hillside, Cody could see the Tatanka warriors clinging to their massive, hunched backs. The riders leant low, one hand gripping the creature's thick mane, the other clutching a long spear.

The Okwaho raced towards the lead bull as if he meant to collide head-on. The rider bolted upright and raised his spear. He cocked his arm and reared back. The Okwaho leapt and sailed through the rain-streaked sky. One arm shot forwards and the other drew back his tomahawk. The buffalo rumbled in beneath him and his feet touched down on the creature's head. He slammed the stone blade of his hatchet down into the shoulder of the buffalo rider, who moved to thrust his spear forwards but crumpled beneath the impact before he could strike.

The rider fell backwards from the buffalo's back. As he slammed against the hillside and rolled down the slope, the wolf pounced on him. The Okwaho bounded across the buffalo's back and leapt to join the melee. The three fighters twisted and tangled like wind-blown shadows. The buffalo dug its hooves into the wet ground, which gave way beneath its weight. The creature slid and skidded, then toppled and tumbled down to the foot of the hill.

The other riders barreled downward and rushed past

Cody, who pressed himself against a large rock. They drove across the open field towards the approaching Okwaho. As the tribes collided, spears and tomahawks flew. On the hillside, the shadowy Okwaho struck at the ground again and again with the blade of his tomahawk. Cody knew the Tatanka warrior lay beneath those blows. He averted his eyes and took a deep breath to steady himself. He feared the Okwaho would come back for him.

Cody scanned the darkness for Eduardo but could not find him. When he spotted the white mare standing motionless about a hundred metres away, he knew it was his best chance. He dashed from behind the rock and ran for the horse. He heard the Okwaho warrior and his wolf howling on the hillside behind him, but didn't look back. He glanced at the battle in the field below, where the Okwaho seemed to be scattering. They ran for the trees as he ran for the mare.

Cody sprinted through the darkness, his boots slipping in the mud. Hard streaks of rain pelted his face. Wind pushed him backwards. The empty pistol holstered at his side banged against his leg. War cries and distant hoof beats echoed. Cody ran. His lungs grew tight. Each breath stung. Injured knee pulsed with pain. Heart beat rapidly. He wiped rain from his eyes.

Focused on the mare, which stood strangely still. Put his head down and ran, hoping to reach the horse before it spooked in the storm and battle. Hoof beats moved towards him. Cody didn't look back. They pounded. The ground shook. Cody ran. He neared the mare. The hoof beats were thunder. Lightning flashed. The mare waited. Cody ran. He leapt and grabbed the saddle horn, pulling himself onto the horse. War cries. The ground shaking. Thunder. Lightning flash. Cody put his heels to the mare.

Stillness.

"Git up!" Cody cried, snapping the reins and setting his heels to the mare once more.

The horse stood bone stiff.

Cody froze.

The only sound now was the wind and the rain. A musty odour carried through the air. A faint shadow stretched across the ground at the mare's hooves. Cody glanced back to find three Tatanka warriors sitting on top of their buffalo watching him.

Slowly he turned to face them. They wore loose buckskin trousers. Dark, leathery skin hung from their broad, high cheekbones and framed their small brown eyes. The tallest of the trio stared intensely. He wiped his finger down the crimson tip of his spear, then smeared the blood from his finger in a line beneath his eyes and across the bridge of his nose. A second warrior, small and wiry, held a buffalo horn and a walnut stick shaved of bark. The third warrior sat closest to Cody. He wore long silver hair and showed the hint of a smile on his dark lips.

"Horse not move," he said, and laughed. The wiry warrior laughed, too, but the tall one only scowled.

Cody didn't respond. He patted the mare's neck. He felt angry that they mocked the fine animal. He wondered what they had done to it.

The silver-haired warrior spoke words Cody did not understand and the tall warrior slid down from his mount and moved towards the mare. He pointed the tip of his spear at Cody as he approached. Cody watched him, barely breathing, his fingers tingling.

The silver-haired warrior waved his hand, and the tall warrior lowered his spear. "Don't fear," he said. "We take the bags and go."

He smiled and Cody nodded.

Still, the tall warrior glared at Cody. He stepped forwards and inspected the saddlebags. Then he reached up and shoved Cody, who flipped out of the saddle, arms flailing, and landed chest down in the mud.

The Tatanka laughed again.

Cody pushed himself up and watched the warrior lift the *mochila* off his saddle.

Something inside stung. Not only had he failed on his first Pony Express ride, but he'd lost Mr Ryder's saddlebags.

The tall warrior passed the bags to the silver-haired one, who inspected the four padlocked pouches. Then he lay the *mochila* across his buffalo's back and looked at Cody.

"Key," he said.

Cody shook his head and held his empty palms forwards. "No key."

The warrior nodded. Then he spoke to the wiry warrior, who tapped his stick against his buffalo horn and chanted. He touched the horn to the mare, and Cody felt the horse relax beneath him.

The Tatanka turned their mounts and lumbered away. The ground shook as they picked up speed, and then gradually settled as they disappeared into the night.

Cody wiped rain from his eyes and called gently for the mare to move. He felt the soft echo of an ache in his heart. In his mind, he saw the barrel of his Colt and the Okwaho warrior and blood. He saw the broken paint mare and the bald man's crimson shirt.

The images mingled and blurred. Cody was both flying from the mare's back and watching the warrior fall. The warrior's eyes showed surprise that he was going to die and held the same disgust as the sheriff's eyes. The warrior's blood seeped through his skin as if it were a shirt.

Cody could feel the Colt's weight in his empty hand. He could feel himself pull the trigger. Feel the gun's power as it jumped back towards him. Hear the crack. See the flash. The drops of crimson falling with the rain. Then he felt himself crying. He knew Pa would tell him to *quit being a sissy*. But he didn't care. He wished Mrs Ryder was there to hold him. He let himself cry.

Eduardo sat beneath the dead tree on the ridge. His chestnut stood a short distance away. A wolf lay at the horse's hooves, dark blood matting a wide patch of fur at its rib cage. The Okwaho lay beside the wolf. Cody couldn't see the warrior's wound, but he knew the contorted body was dead. He wiped rain from his eyes.

Eduardo held a pistol in one hand, his arm resting across his lap. His other hand was pressed against the shoulder of his gun hand. Cody could see blood dripping from beneath the hand. The Okwaho's tomahawk lay beside Eduardo, who both smiled and winced as Cody neared.

"Are you okay?" Cody asked.

"Is your pistol loaded?" Eduardo replied.

Cody unholstered his gun and opened the cylinder. He took a cartridge from his belt, and slipped it into the first hole. As he loaded more bullets, he listened to Eduardo's shallow breathing and stared at the fallen Okwaho. The dead man's knee was turned at an impossible angle and his arm bent back strangely behind his neck. Cody thought of the paint mare struggling to stand and the confused look in its eyes.

"We should go," Eduardo said.

Cody holstered his Colt and helped Eduardo to his feet. "Can you ride?"

"*Si*, a *vaquero* can always ride." Eduardo's broad grin returned for a moment.

Then a man stepped into view. He appeared suddenly, as if the Moon's glow had avoided him one moment and found him the next. His eyes hid in the shadow of his dark, flat-brimmed hat. His square-jawed face was stubbled and weathered. He wore a long brown coat slick with rain, and the heels of his boots jammed the mud as he walked. He seemed to move slowly but covered ground quickly with long strides.

"Not so fast, *hombres*," he said, drawing a shotgun from his coat.

Chapter 15

THE STOLEN MAP

The man stepped forwards and pointed the shotgun at Cody's chest. Lightning flashed, and Cody could see his steel grey eyes set in a hard, unblinking stare. If he breathed, it did not show. His aim, too, was stone still. His finger looked comfortable against the trigger's steel curve, as if he'd pulled it many times before and would not mind to do it again this night.

"I been lookin' for you," the man said finally.

Cody glanced at Eduardo, who watched the stranger intently. "You come to kill me?" he said.

"Could be." The man spat into the rain. "Guess we'll find out soon enough."

Thunder cracked, and Cody jumped, heart pounding. For an instant he thought the shotgun had fired. He took a deep breath and let it out slowly. He touched a hand to his chest, reassured to find no bullet holes. Eduardo and the steel-eyed stranger held dead still, not seeming to notice the boom.

"What do you want from us?" Eduardo said.

"Your friend carries a valuable thing that doesn't belong to him."

"The Tatanka took the saddlebags," Cody said. He pointed down into the valley where he had seen them ride.

"I don't care about your mail bags – and neither do them buffalo riders. They just don't know it." The stranger let go of his shotgun with one hand and raised the brim of his cap so Cody could see his cold grey eyes straight on. "Where's the map, kid?"

Cody stared at the man. He meant to answer, but it was hard to think with the gun aimed at his chest. His heart thumped and his fingers buzzed. His brain felt thick and slow.

"Don't waste my time," the man said. "We talked to your pa. He said you took the map when you robbed Mr King's coach."

"Where's my pa?"

"What do you care?" The stranger laughed. "You're dumb as your old man. Didn't think that was possible."

"I ain't dumb. And neither is my pa." Cody stepped forwards and touched his fingertips to the handle of his Colt.

The man's hand flashed across his shotgun, snapping open one barrel's hammer and then the other. "Fine, kid, he ain't dumb. Now settle down and give me the El Dorado map."

Cody edged backwards. He reached into his pocket and pulled out a wet, crumpled map. He held it out to the stranger who stepped forwards and grabbed it. He glanced down at it, stuffed it in his coat pocket, and shuffled back several steps. Then he raised his shotgun and glared down the barrel at Cody. "Guess what?"

Cody watched the man's finger tense against his trigger.

"I did come to kill you."

"You've got your map," Eduardo said. "Go. No one needs to get hurt."

"Your friend took something of great value to my boss, Mr King. And you killed our savages." The man took another step backwards, the heel of his boot skimming the surface of a dark puddle. "While those savages don't matter much to me, I'd have to say you done us wrong. A boy can't cross a man like Tyrus King and expect to get away with it."

Eduardo raised his pistol and drew back the hammer.

The stranger glanced at him but held his aim on Cody. "I'd set that down if I were you. My partner Morgan is behind them bushes yonder." He gestured with his chin towards a cluster of growth a distance behind the boys. "He's got a long-barreled Winchester rifle trained on you as we speak. And while you probably can't see him, I promise he can hit a gnat's eye in the pitch dark. So set that shooter aside unless you want to join your friend in the grave."

Eduardo didn't flinch. "They'll bury you beside us, *hombre*."

"Morgan," the man hollered. "Fire one off. Show this boy your aim."

Lightning flashed, but no shot came.

"Morgan, dang it!" The man glanced towards the bushes where he expected his partner to be. "Give these boys a taste."

Wind blew and rain fell.

Then hoof beats echoed and a grey horse emerged from the darkness. Smoke! Behind the mustang, on a dark bay mare, rode the old man who had saved Cody from the fire. He aimed a silver pistol at the stranger, who turned and blasted both shotgun barrels towards Smoke and the old man.

Eduardo fired a shot and howled in pain as the recoil jerked his injured arm violently.

The stranger spun and ran. Cody drew his Colt and squeezed the trigger as the man launched himself down the hill. He skidded and tumbled and disappeared into shadow.

The old man climbed from his horse and crouched down beside Eduardo.

Cody raised his gun and cocked the hammer. "What are you doin' to him?"

"Helping him," the old man said. "Just as I helped you." He looked at Cody and raised his white eyebrows as if waiting for a response.

Cody stared at the old man's sparkling green eyes. An image flashed in his mind of the old man standing over him outside the burnt jailhouse. He lowered his Colt and clicked the hammer back into place. "Help him," he said, stepping closer to watch over the man's shoulder. Eduardo looked as pale as a faded ghost.

The old man drew a knife from his belt and cut the bloody shirt away from the boy's wound. The tomahawk had cleaved a deep and jagged gash in Eduardo's flesh. Cody flinched at the sight of the raw opening.

The old man reached inside his jacket and pulled out a small leather pouch and a roll of green leaves. He slid a broad leaf from the roll and spread it on the wet ground. He opened the pouch and poured blue and white flower petals onto the leaf. He pressed the petals flat against the leaf with his thumbs. Then he raised the leaf and pressed it, petals down, into Eduardo's wound.

Eduardo howled as the old man's fingers disappeared into his torn flesh. The old man began to whistle a tune, slow and rising, and the tension eased from Eduardo's slim face. He looked at Cody and grinned, and then fell asleep. The old man took a second leaf and pressed it over the wound. "He'll live for now, but he needs a doctor."

Cody could see the flow of blood had slowed. "Can't you fix him up the rest of the way?" he said.

The old man shook his head. "I've done what I can. Now help me get him up."

He reached behind Eduardo's back and leaned him forwards. Cody stepped forwards and grabbed the boy beneath his good arm, and they lifted him up. Smoke edged forwards and crouched low, presenting the saddle at waist height. Cody and the old man hoisted Eduardo onto the horse's back, behind the saddle. With a nod from the old man, Cody climbed onto the horse.

"I'll wake him enough so he can hang on," the old man said, reaching up and touching Eduardo's cheek.

The injured boy uttered uncomfortable, slumberous murmurings, and leant forwards against Cody's back. With his long fingers he reached up and clutched the collar of Cody's shirt.

They rode through the rain, Cody and Smoke with Eduardo beside the old man on the dark bay mare, and trailed by the white and chestnut Express ponies. As the sun inched into the sky, the clouds and darkness gave way to a red glow that rolled down the hills and skimmed across the tall grass prairies and glinted off ponds and streams and grew bright and golden and shone on a small town in a valley beside a slow-flowing, tree-lined river.

They rode into the town and headed straight to the doctor's office, which the old man knew exactly where to find. The doctor, grey-haired and dark-skinned, reminded Cody of Mr Ryder. After a few words with the old man, he helped them move Eduardo to a bed in his office. The doctor pushed Cody out of the way and inspected the wound.

"You boys a little young to play so rough," he said.

"Okwaho," the old man told him.

The doctor raised his eyebrows. "I see," he said, lifting a thin blade from a nearby table.

"We'll let you do your work," the old man said, sidling to the doorway.

Cody did not move. He had only known Eduardo a single night, but he felt they were friends. And he felt that what had happened to the boy was his fault. He stood and watched the doctor clean the leaves away from Eduardo's wound. His feet wouldn't move. He felt it would be wrong to leave.

Finally the doctor looked up at Cody. He stared into his eyes and smiled. "He's going to be fine," he said. "Go get some breakfast."

Cody nodded, "Tell him I said thanks," and followed the old man out into the morning.

Chapter 16

FORGETTING

Cody felt exhausted but didn't try to sleep. He sat on the dirt, staring at the river, listening to the water gurgle over the rocks. In his mind, he saw a bullet from his gun rip into the Okwaho's chest. A spray of crimson blood in the moonlight. The warrior's face contorted with pain and surprise. His amber eyes as he fell, locked on Cody's eyes.

Cody tried to force the memory away, but the image flashed in his mind again and again. His head felt numb and slow. His limbs tingled. The tangled knot in his stomach clenched like a fist. With one decision, one squeeze of the trigger, he had ended a man's life. He felt raw and withered inside. But some shadowed place in him felt capable and strong. He had bested another man in the ultimate confrontation. He had emerged uninjured from a night-long battle that left Eduardo bloodied and the fat man dead. He felt superior, and it troubled him.

Cody put his face in his hands and squeezed his eyes shut. The image continued to repeat itself, pounding down on him like drops of rain in a storm. He thought about bashing his head against the rock that jutted from the river so the memory would float away with his blood. He opened his eyes and shivered.

The old man sat down beside him. He patted Cody's back and sighed. He drew his knees towards his chest and draped his arms across them. He stared out at the river and whistled softly.

Cody watched the old man gazing at the river. "I ain't killed a man before," he said.

The old man nodded and gazed at the water.

"I know he tried to kill Eduardo," Cody said. He pressed his lips together tightly, determined not to cry. "But maybe he had a son. Maybe I killed some boy's pa."

"That may be."

Cody clenched his teeth and looked down at his hand, the finger that pulled the trigger. His whole body tightened. "That don't make me feel no better."

"You killed a man. You ought to feel bad for a time. Take it as a good sign." He offered the hint of a smile.

"I'm not saying you made the wrong choice. But killing a man has consequences. You shouldn't forget that."

Cody nodded and looked out at the water. He thought about how small a bullet was compared to a river, how it could get pulled away so easily in the current.

"You planning to sleep, son?"

Cody shook his head. "Don't think I could."

The old man looked at Cody and put his hand on his shoulder. The he hopped to his feet. "Come on," he said.

The old man stood in the river up to his knees. He held a fishing pole in each hand. Cody followed him reluctantly into the cold water. "Ain't we gonna spook the fish?"

"Just try not to fall in." He handed Cody a pole.

Cody studied the length of bamboo in his hand. It was different than what he normally used to fish, a stick with a line tied to the end. This pole stretched a good ten feet long with a series of metal hoops fastened along one side. The fishing line ran through the loops and wrapped around a metal wheel, which was attached at the thicker end of the pole.

The old man waited as Cody examined the pole.

Then he showed him how to pull line from the metal wheel, which he called a reel, and turn the handle to wind it back up. "That's how you haul in a fish," he said. He called the pole a rod and showed Cody a hook with small black and tan feathers tied to it. "This is the fly," he said. "Looks pretty close to what you'll find flitting around this river."

Cody had never seen a hook decorated that way. He always dug up worms and twisted them onto a plain hook. Best way to catch blues and sunnies.

The old man showed Cody how to pull some line and cast it out. It took a few tries, but Cody started to get the hang of it. He held the rod straight up and titled it back over his shoulder. Then he thrust it forwards and the line with the fly on it sailed out and dropped into the river. Cody watched the line floating on the water's easy current.

"How we gonna catch any fish if the hook don't sink?" he said.

"If you tease 'em right, they'll come to the hook."

Cody eyed the hook sceptically as it drifted downstream.

"When your fly comes back to this side, reel it in and cast it across," the man told him. "I'll be upstream a bit."

Cody reeled in his line and cast it again into the river.

He watched the line float on the slow water. He watched the water slip and splash over the glassy rocks. He watched the sun dance on the water's shifting surface and the pines and poplars sway in the breeze. He heard the wind glide across leaves and felt the cold river slide around his legs. He heard birds calling to one another before soaring through the sky. He took a deep breath. His legs felt numb from the cold, but his head began to clear. His hands felt comfortable at work on the rod and reel. He forgot.

Up ahead, set against blue sky and billowy clouds, the old man whipped his line high above his head. He swept it one way and then the other in graceful, looping arcs and let it fall slowly to the water. He worked back and forth across the river, watching the water intently. Cody, himself, began to notice winged bugs flitting between the water's surface and the sky. He could see small ripples blossom on the water where the fish were feeding. He began to understand.

The old man worked steadily in smooth flowing motions, the line floating through the sky like a ribbon in the wind. Then he paused, and Cody could feel what was about to happen. A plop and a splash. The old man jerked the rod and began to reel in the slack. The rod bowed sharply, and he leaned his weight back. A long, colourful trout leapt out of the water, thrashing its head and twisting its body in the air. The old man dropped his rod tip into the water and pulled it back out as the fish splashed down. Then he reeled and leaned, reeled and leaned, until the tired fish was within his reach. He lifted his catch out of the water with one hand, still holding the line taut with the other, and walked carefully to the riverbank.

"Come on out," he said to Cody. "Breakfast time."

The old man showed Cody how to gut the fish and pull out the spine and skeleton. Then they started a fire and set the fillet in a pan to cook. Cody sat in the dirt with his back against a rock. The old man sat on a fallen tree trunk. Smoke and the bay slept in the shade of the nearby pines.

"What's your name, son?" the old man said. "Seems we've been through too much not to know each others' names."

"I'm Cody, and that horse you gave me is called Smoke."

The old man smiled. "Fitting name."

Cody nodded. The smell from the cooking trout made his stomach groan.

"I'm called Bart."

Cody regarded the man's round face and his sparkling

green eyes. "How'd you know to show up last night? And why do you keep helping me?"

Bart tipped back his bowler, the hint of a smile on his lips. "You seem to need a lot of help."

Cody frowned.

"Plus," Bart said, reaching forwards with a fork to flip the trout, "Smoke's got a nose for these things."

Cody glanced at the sleeping horse. He wondered if Bart would try to take the mustang back when he left.

Bart looked up from the trout, which sizzled in the hot pan. "Tell me, son. Did the bandit take the El Dorado map?"

Cody felt his body tighten. "How'd you know about the map? You aim to take it from me if he didn't?"

"I don't have any interest in owning the map, if that's what you mean."

Cody looked in the old man's eyes, and nothing had changed. Pa always said a man's eyes would change if you remind him he's lying. So Cody decided the old man spoke truthfully. "He took a map," Cody said, "but not the El Dorado map." He could feel a smile creasing his lips, despite his efforts to look serious. "I gave him a Pony Express map, and I guess he couldn't tell the difference."

Bart grinned and his eyes sparkled. "Clever."

"He called me dumb, and he called my pa dumb," Cody said. "I didn't much like it. We ain't dumb."

"I guess you're not."

Bart took the fish from the pan and set it on two tin plates. It didn't taste quite as good as Mrs Ryder's cooking, but it still tasted better than most breakfasts Cody ate. Maybe it had something to do with how good it felt to be alive just then. After he ate all his fish, Cody drank from the river. Then he sat back against the rock and closed his eyes.

"I liked fishing in the river," he said.

"I'm glad," Bart said. "Now get some sleep."

When Cody woke, the sun was setting beyond the river. It tinted the water and sky fiery orange. To Cody, it looked like the world might burn up at any moment.

Bart was gone and Cody walked down to the water hoping to find him there fishing. When he didn't see him, he decided to check the woods, figuring Bart was collecting firewood or plants like the ones he used to patch up Eduardo's wound. Smoke and the bay stood chewing some bushes at the edge of the clearing, so Bart couldn't have gone far.

Cody moved slowly through the pines and poplars. His muscles ached, and he still felt tired. He didn't need to find the old man, but he wanted to be near him. He feared that the images would return. Somehow it seemed that the old man had eased them.

Cody wondered how Eduardo was doing. The doctor must have finished sewing him up hours ago. He hoped they could visit him during the evening. Cody wanted to fish again, too, but that would have to wait until morning.

As he reached the edge of the trees, Cody heard voices. He crept forwards quietly and strained to hear. One voice belonged to Bart; the other sounded familiar, too. He couldn't recall who it belonged to, but it gave him an uneasy feeling. He crouched down and crept low behind the bushes and tree trunks. He eased through the woods, stepping as slowly and quietly as possible. When he got close enough that he could make out the words being spoken, Cody raised himself to see above the brush line.

Bart stood in the prairie grass talking to the three Tatanka warriors. "The boy has the map," he said.

Cody's fingers started to tingle.

Chapter 17

OUTLAW

The two bamboo fishing rods leant against the trunk of a thick, old poplar tree. Cody gazed at them and thought about how quiet and beautiful the world seemed when he cast his line out into the river – and how Bart had seemed so kind and generous. He should have known better than to trust the old man. Nobody helps you like that unless he wants something from you. Bart was even worse than Pa, because Pa, at least, never hid who he was or what he wanted.

Cody bent forwards and took up the rods in his hands. On the ground by the tree was a canvas bag and cloth ties. Cody dismantled the rods into smaller pieces, put them in the bag, and tied them to the back of his saddle. He glanced around the camp one last time and climbed onto Smoke's back.

"Come on, Smoke," he said. "We gotta go."

The horse nickered and shuffled a step backwards.

"No messin' around. Let's go." Cody set his heels to the horse's flanks and the two set off on their own again. They rode hard for a time, then found a low riffle where they could ford the river. There the pine trees grew thicker and provided enough cover that they could slow their pace. Cody gave Smoke the reins so the mustang could recover from the run. He knew Bart and the Tatanka would follow, but he didn't think they would find him if he kept moving. He would go to El Dorado himself. He would get the gold from the city and live like a king. Buy a dozen fishing rods and a plot of land along a quiet river. Take care of himself. He wouldn't need Pa, or Bart, or even the Ryders.

The sky was darkening, but Cody intended to ride through until morning. A full Moon hung brightly in the blue night and would guide the way. Cody reached into his pocket and fished out the El Dorado map. He unfolded it and held it up to the moonlight. The golden sun had reappeared near the south-western edge of the Freelands.

Cody was puzzling over the changing map when the first shot blasted. A second shot quickly followed and showered bark and wood chips from a nearby tree onto the brim of his hat.

"Did I tell you Morgan could shoot?" called a gravelly voice that Cody recognized instantly as belonging to the stranger with the shotgun. "Stay right there, kid, or the next one's in your head."

Cody felt pretty certain the man meant what he said and reined Smoke to a stop.

A moment later, the stranger stepped onto the trail. His tall frame seemed always to be etched in shadow.

In the woods along the trail, Cody heard twigs snapping and the yipping of wolves. He gazed into the shadowy tree line trying to spot the Okwaho. He couldn't see them, but he knew they were there.

The stranger tipped up the brim of his hat and smiled. "As you've gathered, we're not alone," he said. "This time I brought savages." He pushed his long coat back so it caught behind his holsters, leaving a clear path from his hands to his six-guns. Cody didn't bother reaching for his own pistol.

"What happened to your friends?" the man said. His voice held a trace of laughter.

"Eduardo's at the doc's, and I ain't got no other friends except this horse." Cody set his jaw tightly and glared at the stranger.

"Ain't you tough?" the man said. "Got to admit that was a clever trick giving me the wrong map. Guess you ain't as dumb as your pa."

"You took the wrong map," Cody said. "How dumb's that make you?"

Now the stranger laughed deeply. "I like you, kid. Clever is good, and you ain't yellow neither. Why don't you ride with me?"

Cody watched the man, waiting for the joke.

"Name's Gus Grimshaw," the man said. "Ever heard of me?"

"I seen a wanted poster."

"I suppose it wasn't as handsome as the real thing."

Now Cody laughed, and Gus Grimshaw laughed too.

"What do you say, kid? We got plenty of work. I'll give you a fair cut."

Something didn't feel right. This man almost killed him last night. Now he wanted to be partners. Cody looked at Gus's steel eyes but couldn't read his intention.

Gus smiled and flipped his long coat back over his holsters. "Come on kid, I could use the company.

Morgan ain't much for talkin'. And savages is savages."

Cody considered Gus, who didn't seem as angry as Pa. And he liked the way Gus laughed a lot. "You ain't gonna kill me?" he said.

The outlaw laughed hoarsely and spat. "Why would I kill a kid who was riding with me?"

Cody shrugged. "Hard to say."

"Well, don't test me." Gus smiled, but didn't laugh. Then he stepped forwards and held out a hand to Cody. They shook. When Gus let go, Cody drew his arm back, but Gus kept his open hand raised towards the boy. "The map," he said.

Cody reached into his pocket and pulled out the old, folded paper. As he raised it towards the outlaw's hand, a gold coin fell from the fold. Cody watched the coin drop through the air and land on the trail. It clinked against a small rock as it settled in the dirt.

Gus watched the coin fall, too. He raised his eyebrows at Cody, then bent down and picked up the shining gold piece. He turned the coin in his hand and studied it. "Ain't King's," he said, and held it out to Cody, who regarded it but did not move to take it. He had forgotten the coins were in his pocket.

"Go on. Take it," Gus said. "I ain't gonna steal my partner's gold."

Cody took the coin, and Gus took the map.

"This map is a different story," he said. "It ain't yours. But that coin is yours."

Cody looked down at the coin and rubbed his thumb across its face. The knot in his stomach uncoiled and shook. He remembered raising the piano lid and sticking his hand in the sack of coins. Then he thought about playing the piano with Mrs Ryder. He could almost feel the music swelling from inside. Sad music. It somehow reminded him of fishing the river. He wished he could feel good like that now. Sunshine. Water bubbling over rocks. The line floating through the air and drifting with the current. He wished he could be there now and forget that he had stolen from the Ryders. He wished he could go to El Dorado and start a new life. The knot in his stomach writhed like an injured snake.

Morgan's rifle stood nearly as tall as he did. His thick, black moustache covered his mouth, which was straight and tight. He walked two dappled grey ponies out of the woods and handed a set of reins to Gus before climbing aboard the second horse.

A single Okwaho emerged behind the rifleman.

Streaks of crimson marked his cheeks and he eyed Cody darkly. He stepped up to Gus and grabbed his arm. He whispered curtly, motioning towards Cody with his head and glowering.

Gus turned sharply towards the Okwaho, spinning the man so they faced each other. Gus's eyes bore down on him severely. He shook his head slowly. The Okwaho glared at Cody and stomped back into the woods.

Gus watched him go and laughed. "Don't worry about him," he said. "Unpleasant is their natural disposition."

They set off at an easy pace and Cody wondered if Bart would catch them. The sky darkened and the moon seemed to glow more brightly. The breeze slid coolly through the night and Cody listened to the leaves rustle as the Okwaho and their wolves moved through the shadowed woods.

Gus glanced at Cody from time to time, smirking as if acknowledging some private joke between them. "So you ever rob a coach?" he said.

Cody nodded.

"That was a trick question." Gus held up the map. "I knew you did. How about a shop?"

Cody nodded.

"A bank?"

"Once."

"A train?"

Cody shook his head.

"We'll work on that." Gus grinned and nodded approvingly. "I have to say, you've got a lot of experience for a kid. What's the worst job you ever pulled?"

Cody looked down at the dark trail. He thought about the Ryders' piano and the feel of the coins as he reached inside the sack. "I don't want to say."

"You got to say."

Cody shook his head.

Gus grabbed Cody's shoulder and turned him in his saddle. His steely eyes, suddenly serious, bore down on Cody. "You've got to say."

Cody pulled his shoulder way, and Gus let it go.

"I robbed my friends," Cody said. "They put me up. But when I had to go, I needed money for the road. And I took it from them."

"Whoo hee!" Gus called. "Robbed your friends. I am impressed. You're a born outlaw!"

He grinned widely and shook his head.

Cody rubbed his thumb across the face of the gold coin.

Chapter 18

POSSIBILITY

As the night dragged on, Cody drifted behind his new companions. Smoke seemed resistant to riding too close to the men and their dappled ponies, and Cody felt more comfortable with some distance between them. He could see them up ahead, but in the dim moonlight they appeared as black shadows cut from the dark sky. The rise of Morgan's rifle loomed above the man, as he never lowered the weapon or tied it to his saddle like most riders. Gus Grimshaw rode tall and still in his saddle, and Cody wondered what he thought about during those long, horse-bound hours.

From the treetops, bats rose skywards and swarmed like storm clouds to swallow the mosquitoes that flitted through the moonlight and nipped at Cody's neck and the back of his hands. He swung his hat at the insects from time to time, but mostly tried to ignore them. The night felt warm, though a strong breeze sent a chill through Cody when it poured over the trail. The wind carried the calls of distant owls marking their territory, and crows cawed as if in response. Cody could hear the Okwaho, too, lurking beyond the tree line. Twigs cracking. Leaves rustling. Wolves growling faintly.

When this subtle drone of these hidden travellers ceased, Cody knew something was wrong. Smoke knew it too. The mustang tensed and quickened its pace, but Cody reined the horse to a halt. He closed his eyes and listened. The buzzing mosquitoes and fluttering bats subsided to the back of his perception as he focused on the Okwaho. Their silence became an empty space in the night's dark hum. In that hole, Cody could hear his heart beat. Hear himself breathing. Feel his fingers tingle. He feared the void might swallow his soul if he listened too long. Then, barely audible, a foot scuffed the dirt behind him. Cody spun and drew his Colt.

An Okwaho stood in the trail. His form was less visible than shadow, like something imagined. Cody couldn't see him so much as sense him. He couldn't see the smear of blood on the warrior's cheek, but he knew the man wore one. He couldn't see the man move, but he felt him grow closer. He perceived the dark form of a wolf skulking at his feet, a prowling shadow. He perceived the tomahawk clutched in the man's hand, the stone blade waiting to be loosed in the night and plunged into Cody's skull. He felt the rage boiling in the pit of the warrior's stomach.

In the half-sight of darkness, the forms seemed very still while the world bent like vapour, sliding them forwards. Cody raised his Colt towards the Okwaho. He knew the man would kill him. He set his thumb against the gun's steel hammer and drew it back. It clicked loudly. Then his senses went wild. The sound of his pounding heartbeat rose to his ears. He could feel the stiff sole of his boot pressing against the bottom of his foot, the fabric of his shirtsleeve brushing his skin, the tightness of his hat around his head. A buzz of nerves rushed over him like a river set free from a dam. His face grew damp with sweat. The frenzy in his chest radiated through his body. The knot in his stomach uncoiled and churned. His hands went numb. He could no longer feel the cold hard trigger against his finger. A crow cawed.

Cody heard the warrior's feet skating quickly over the trail. He tried to pull the trigger, but his hand wouldn't respond. In his mind, he saw the Okwaho at the Express outpost, blood spurting from his chest. His amber eyes as he fell. The paint mare, falling. The man from the stagecoach, a blotch of crimson spreading over his white shirt. He heard the silence of those moments, the emptiness. He felt the pause between his wild heart beats. He opened his eyes and saw the Okwaho running through the silence, the dark wolf gliding beside him. He felt his eyes blink. He inhaled. He realized he was going to die. He exhaled. A wonderful breeze slid across his cheeks. He wondered if he'd see his mother.

Two shots blasted. Cody felt himself snap from his haze. The Okwaho and the wolf tumbled to a stop where Smoke stood. Cody could smell the wildness of the man and the iron tinge of his blood.

Gus Grimshaw appeared then as if he had formed from the darkness. He arrived almost instantly, yet seemed to move slowly. He held a six-gun in each hand, and glowered as his steely eyes scanned the darkness. "I will gut every last one of you savages if you come near this boy again," he hollered. "I will slaughter your wolves and stew them with carrots."

Grimshaw waited for a response, which did not come, then set his guns back in their holsters.

"What happened, kid? I saw you turn on him, but you never fired."

Cody looked at the pistol in his hand. It felt like it didn't belong there. He slipped it into his holster. "Jammed."

Grimshaw stared at him and frowned. "You better ride closer."

Cody pulled up alongside the two riders as they set off again. He looked at Morgan, who glanced at Cody then set his eyes straight ahead.

"Thanks," Cody said. "For making the shot. It was you, right?"

Morgan said nothing.

"Don't thank him," Grimshaw said. "He'd have shot you, too, if I told him."

Cody didn't look at Grimshaw. He set his eyes forwards and rode through the night. He wondered what would have happened if he had died. He'd seen death before, but never had the possibility of his own death seemed so close. It made him think of the Ryders, and all the possibility he saw in their lives. Mrs Ryder loved to create music, and Mr Ryder loved to build saddles. And they loved each other. What, Cody wondered, did he love?

He thought about what life would be like for the Ryders' baby. He imaged a little girl who would dance while Mrs Ryder played the piano. She would cling to Mr Ryder's back and he would carry her to the river where they'd picnic and laugh. And when she grew tall and beautiful, she would go to school and become a doctor or a teacher or a shopkeeper. There would be lots of hugs along the way, and her parents would be proud of her always.

Cody knew it was too late for him to have those things, but he wondered what he would miss if he died, if better things might come to him some day. He wondered if anyone would miss him like he missed his ma. He wondered how his life might be different if she hadn't died giving birth to him. Maybe he deserved his troubles for starting his life that way. But he never meant for it to happen. He wished he could tell her that.

⊙~⊙

"How'd you end up ridin' with Black Bart?" Grimshaw held a strip of jerky out to Cody, who took it and ripped off a piece using his back teeth.

"Black Bart?"

Grimshaw shook his head. "You never heard of Black Bart – the no-good, yellow-bellied bandit you been ridin' with?"

"I heard of Black Bart, but I didn't know the old man was him," Cody said. He thought about how Bart had double-crossed him with the buffalo riders. "Guess I'm not surprised."

Grimshaw raised his eyebrows and gave a sideways nod.

In truth, Cody did feel surprised – and disappointed. Even though he had left Bart behind, some part of Cody still hoped the old man really cared about him. He had saved Cody twice. And if he didn't care about him, then why did he do it? Couldn't he have taken the map more easily if Cody were dead?

"Guess it suits you, hangin' out with vermin." Grimshaw smiled. "Your pa's a mean cuss."

Morgan laughed.

Cody shot the rifleman a dirty look. "He's my pa. What choice do I have?"

Grimshaw sniggered and shook his head. "No argument here. I'd rather have your pa fighting with me than fighting against me."

Cody felt like there was a question to ask, but it wouldn't come to his mind. He set his eyes forwards and rode on. He patted Smoke's neck and listened to the clopping of the horses' hooves. He watched the darkness lift from the sky like a dissolving shadow. He thought about Pa and the choices ahead of him. He had never before considered that he had choices, that he had possibility. He patted Smoke's neck and rode on.

CHAPTER 19

A BEND IN THE RIVER

"I guess it's thirty-two men I killed." Gus Grimshaw paused and glanced at both Morgan and Cody before adding, "not counting savages." Then he laughed deeply. Morgan joined in, his head and chest bobbing with laughter though no sound escaped his lips.

Grimshaw, who spat when he laughed, wiped his mouth with the back of his hand. "Should I count 'em if Morgan pulled the trigger?" Their laughter resumed and deepened until Grimshaw stopped abruptly and glared at Cody. He wiped his mouth again. "You don't laugh no more?"

Cody felt Grimshaw's steely eyes bearing down on him. He leant away in his saddle and glanced at Grimshaw's hands. The man's long, weathered fingers curled around his reins loosely. Cody felt his own hands tighten on his reins. "Just tired," he said.

Grimshaw scowled. "I forget why I brought you along," he said. "You don't laugh. Can't kill a savage. You ain't no fun, boy."

Cody watched the man but didn't respond.

Grimshaw shook his head. "We're almost to the Skyscraper. You can sleep then. Maybe it'll liven you up."

Cody had heard of skyscrapers in big eastern cities. He had even seen a drawing of one, twenty stories high, rising above the other buildings. But he didn't think there were any cities big enough for such a building this far west.

Soon, the trees thinned and the land grew flat and brown as the party emerged from the forest and onto a plain that extended far into the distance. They rode across the open space for some time, dust rising from the horses' hooves. The sun glared down harshly, and sweat dripped from the band of Cody's hat down the sides of his face. His damp shirt clung to his back and his feet smouldered in his boots. He felt thankful for the wide brim of his grey hat, which kept the sun out of his eyes and off of his nose. He sipped from his canteen to wet his dry lips.

Far off, a mountain range stretched across the

horizon and reached into the clouds. At the mid-point of the range stood a tall and lonesome structure. Cody could barely make out the form in the distance, but he knew it must be the Skyscraper.

Ten Okwaho warriors and their wolves trailed the three riders. Even in the wide open space, their movements seemed dangerous and skulking. Cody felt thankful to have some distance between them.

He reached down and patted Smoke's hot, sweaty neck. "You can rest soon," he said.

Then he felt the slightest tremble in the baked dirt beneath them. He knew what was coming before it happened. The vibration rose and built until the ground pulsed and shook. The sound of it boomed across the vast space. A cloud of dirt burst from the shade of the forest and swept across the plain in an arced path, careening towards them like a sudden storm. Cody could see the dark shapes of the Tatanka warriors and their enormous mounts within the dusty billow. He looked for Bart but couldn't find the old man.

Grimshaw and Morgan stopped and turned. Grimshaw shouted at the Okwaho, who spun and set themselves at a hard charge towards their enemies. The two tribes clashed on the plain in an earthy haze. The Okwaho raced and leapt, attacked and rolled away. The wolves darted between the warriors, jaws wide, teeth flashing. The Tatanka leant tightly against the backs of their mounts, stabbing with their spears. The buffalo rumbled forwards, heads down, eyes wild.

A screaming Okwaho sprang high into the air and flipped forwards, landing with one foot on the back of a buffalo, just behind its rider. He touched down only an instant before leaping upwards, seeming to float there above the charging beasts. He clawed at the first rider with one hand and thrust his stone-bladed tomahawk towards the second. The riders ducked and blocked. The first swung his spear in a spiralling arc above his head and behind his back, catching the wolf warrior with the sharp end as his foot touched down on the second buffalo's back. The warrior swayed slowly backwards, then slid off the spear end, dropping to the ground and bouncing limply across the dirt as the battle raced forwards.

Gus Grimshaw turned his horse and called back to Cody. "Let's ride!"

Cody watched Grimshaw and Morgan set their spurred heels to their horses' ribs. The two mounts lurched forwards in unison, kicking up a plume of dust behind them. Cody reined Smoke in their direction but hesitated to follow. He scanned the vast plain, and found himself hoping Bart would emerge from the skirmish. He looked for the old man's dark bay and black bowler hat. His sparkling green eyes.

Instead he saw an Okwaho scamper along the ground then suddenly rise upright into a full sprint. The Tatanka warrior ahead of him reared back and cocked his arm above his head. Then his whole body snapped forwards like the hammer of a gun. A spear flew from his hand towards the belly of the racing Okwaho. Cody turned away before the weapon made impact, but in his mind he heard the slitting sound as the sharp tip of the spear tore through the man's flesh. He saw crimson spurt from the tight space between the wooden shaft and the flesh where it had impaled itself. He saw the warrior's eyes grow wide with the sudden realization he was going to die.

Cody knew then that he couldn't follow Grimshaw. Death should not be unleashed so easily. He turned Smoke halfway between the outlaws and the battle. "Git up!" he called, setting his heels to the grey mustang. The horse showed its strength, leaping from a dead stop into a full gallop. Cody felt some small relief ease into his limbs. He wasn't safe yet, he knew, but he had finally made a right choice. He would get away from everyone – the Okwaho and Tatanka, Grimshaw and Morgan, even Bart. Maybe he couldn't go to El Dorado now, but he would find somewhere quiet to live, somewhere near a river. For the briefest moment, he wondered where Pa had gone. Then he heard a voice calling to him.

"Cody!" Grimshaw hollered. "I can't let you go." He had stopped and turned towards the boy. Morgan pulled up beside the outlaw and tucked the butt of his rifle against his shoulder.

Cody leant forwards in his saddle. "Run, Smoke! Run!" He could feel the horse push harder, the beat of its hooves blurring into a single, long roll. Then a distant shot fired and Cody's body tensed. His eyes darted towards the outlaws and he saw a small grey bullet speeding towards him. He knew it wasn't possible, but he could see the bullet approach. He heard a sound like a hurricane and the rounded head of the slug began to vibrate. The air surrounding it became visible, like a vapour. It bent and curled against the bullet, which slowed and shook and warbled. Finally, an arm's length from Cody's chest, it stalled. It hung in the air a split second – and Cody thought to reach out and catch it – before it fell to the ground.

He exhaled as a second shot blasted. Again, he watched the lead slug hurtle towards him and slow against the wind. This time, he didn't wait for the bullet to stop. He snapped his reins and set his heels to the mustang's ribs. "Git up!" he called, and Smoke burst into a furious gallop.

Cody pulled his hat from his head and clutched it in his fist. Smoke lowered his head and ran. They raced across the plain, a spray of dirt trailing behind them. Smoke ran straight for a long stretch then veered towards a distant stand of cottonwood trees. Cody crouched low and worked his legs in rhythm with the mustang's movement. As they reached the trees, he glanced back but saw no one in the open space behind them. Once inside the cover of the trees, Smoke slowed and Cody eased himself upright and set his hat back on. They rode through the small woods and emerged on a wide stretch of rocky dirt and scrub grass.

The land rose gently for a long span and they followed it skywards. Broad patches of pale rock surfaced from the drab soil, and Cody listened to the sharp clopping of Smoke's hooves on the hard surface. Finally, they reached a low ridge and Cody reined Smoke to a stop. They had been travelling a long time, and the mustang had slowed noticeably. Cody dismounted and opened his canteen. He found a cleft in a smooth outcropping of rock, took a drink from the canteen and poured the rest of the water into the hollow. Smoke leant in and drank and Cody patted the grey's sweaty neck. He gazed down the incline they had just climbed. Except for the rocks and low grass, the stretch was bare. Cody could see all the way back to the cottonwoods where they had started. If anyone was following, he would have seen them. They were safe for the time, he decided.

Ahead, the ridge sloped down more steeply and, eventually, met with a density of pines and maples that stretched widely. Cody started walking down the slope. He hoped they could reach the tree cover by nightfall.

"Come on, friend," he said, and Smoke followed. They walked slowly down the hill. Cody's muscles ached, and he felt nauseated from lack of sleep. From time to time, he stopped to make sure no one was following, but the land sat still and quiet. The only movement came from a lone hawk, which soared overhead and circled them once before gliding back towards the plain.

As the sun set somewhere far beyond the forest, they reached the tree line and ventured into the woods. They moved slowly as there was no obvious path through the thick growth. Cody felt pleased to be out of the hot sun, but less pleased to meet the swarms of mosquitoes and gnats that greeted them. He waved his hat incessantly and uselessly as they pressed deeper into the woods. His neck, hands and ears were soon pocked with itchy welts.

Then the woods grew dark as moonlight replaced the sunlight. Cody looked for a clearing where they could spend the night and was soon rewarded with the sound of gurgling water.

"Come on, Smoke," he said. "A little longer and we can rest."

Ahead they found a small river, which they followed downstream until the water slowed and collected in a low, lazy pool. There, the trees opened on a small clearing, and a patch of tall grass abutted an incline of damp, pebbled dirt that eased into the water.

Cody threw his hat into the grass, crawled up to the pool, and stuck his head in the cool water. Smoke stepped up to the water beside him. They both drank deeply.

Cody felt hungry, but even more tired. He decided he could eat in the morning. He lay down in the dirt and closed his eyes. For the briefest moment, he wondered where he was heading. Then he fell into a deep sleep. Smoke stood beside him and did the same.

◯～◯

When he woke, Cody found a campfire burning within a small circle of rocks arranged on the damp dirt.

He sat up abruptly and gripped the walnut handle of his Colt, lifting the gun from its holster. Smoke, already awake, stood calmly chewing a pine sapling. Cody shook his head irritably at the horse. He moved towards the fire, stepping as quietly as he could, turning in a circle and scanning the forest as he moved. Beside the fire stood a pair of black boots, and beside them began a set of footprints leading into the river. He followed the prints to the water's edge, his gun hand extended chest-high. He could see downstream easily enough, but found no one. His upstream view was blocked by a sharp bend in the river. He slipped off his boots and waded in, shivering as the chilly water rushed over the skin of his legs. He moved slowly, trying not to slosh. The current tugged at his feet. Finally, he was able to peer around the thick growth of the riverbank, and there, just beyond the bend, he found Bart, waist-deep in the water, reeling in a cast with one of the rods Cody had taken from him.

He glanced at Cody and smiled. His green eyes twinkled in the morning sunlight. "Glad you're up," he said. "We've got some nice trout for breakfast."

Chapter 20

BREAKFAST

The sun shone brightly now and weaved treetop shadows across the clearing where Cody and Bart sat. The smell of the campfire and cooking fish and damp earth mingled in the cool fresh morning air. Bart whistled while he cooked. His melody mingled with the sound of water gurgling and birds singing and soft breezes shifting tall lengths of grass. Cody watched him and scowled.

He kept remembering Bart standing with the Tatanka at the edge of the woods. Then he could see Bart's hand gripping his own hand outside the charred jailhouse. And he could see Pa's hand flicking the unlit matchstick through the cell's barred window. In his mind, the images overlapped as if they had occurred in the same moment.

Now, Bart handed Cody a tin plate with a charred trout and half a red apple on it. Cody grabbed the plate and began shovelling the fish into his mouth with his fingers. He felt too hungry to cut it or use a fork – or even chew it. He shovelled until all the fish on the plate was gone. Then he chomped the apple in three large mouthfuls. He licked his fingers for anything he might have missed.

Bart watched him and smiled pleasantly as if he hadn't wronged Cody in any manner, which made Cody angry. He just couldn't decide what to make of the old man. Pa would have said, *If you ain't sure, don't trust him. And if you are, don't trust him anyway.* But somehow that didn't feel right to Cody.

"I'll cook you some more fish after you've had time to digest," Bart said. "But sorry, no more apples." He took a bite from his own apple slice and smiled. One cheek puffed full with the sweet fruit as he mashed it with his back teeth.

Cody grunted in what he thought a neutral sound, so as not to turn down the offer but not express any appreciation either.

Bart nodded as if this was a perfectly acceptable answer. He ate the rest of his breakfast slowly, using a fork to cut and handle the trout.

Cody felt no surprise people called this double-crossing old man Black Bart. He glared at him, wondering what things Bart had done to earn such a name. Pa had been an outlaw since before Cody was born and no one even knew his name. Bart must be the worst of the bad. So why did he act like Cody's friend?

The old man's green eyes glinted. His pale lips curled with the hint of a smile. He whistled between bites of trout.

"I ain't got the map no more," Cody said finally. "So you can stop being nice."

Bart nodded. "I thought as much."

"Then what are you doin' here?" Cody said, his voice rising. The muscles in his face tightened. He felt a sudden anger burning in his chest. He exhaled sharply and threw his hat towards the fire.

Bart snatched the grey hat from the air before it reached the flames. He ran his fingers along the brim. "That's a fine hat," he said. "You shouldn't toss it away for no reason."

He flipped it back and Cody caught it. He glared at Bart and balled his hand into a fist, crumpling the hat's brim in his fingers. He felt a heap of words caught at the back of his throat but he couldn't get them out. He exhaled sharply and squeezed his fist tighter.

Bart looked straight into Cody's eyes and held his gaze until Cody unclenched his hand. "Son, what do you think stopped those bullets?"

Cody's eyebrows rose.

Bart leant in towards him, his green eyes unblinking.

"That was you?" Cody said.

"Son, I don't want any harm to come to you. Understand?"

Cody nodded and Bart lay another trout fillet into the pan and set it on the fire to cook.

"What is it you think I did to you, son? What's got you so riled up?"

"I seen you with them buffalo riders." Cody watched the thin meat frying in the pan. Little sparks of grease flew up as it sizzled. "They been tryin' to kill me and you meant to hand me over."

Bart slid his fork under the fish and scrapped the pan in short jerky movements to unstick the meat from the hot wrought iron. Then he flipped it over and looked at Cody. "The Tatanka did follow you, son. But they weren't going to kill you. They were chasing the map, which belongs to them in the first place."

"A treasure map belongs to whoever finds it."

Bart shook his head. "That map belongs to the Tatanka. El Dorado is Tatanka tribal land."

"Tribal land?"

"Since the earth was born." Bart took Cody's empty plate from him.

"Is it really made of gold?"

"So to speak. And the day the wrong man finds El Dorado, the Tatanka will lose everything. Men like King and Grimshaw would take everything."

Cody thought of Pa. He knew Bart was right. "Have you been there?"

"I have. It's beautiful, but not magnificent in the way you might think. The Tatanka live there. Their children play there. It's a home."

"But most men won't see it that way," Cody said.

Bart shook his head. "They won't." He set the cooked trout on a plate and passed it to Cody.

This time Cody waited for Bart to hand him a fork. He stabbed the white meat and raised it into his mouth. He chewed and watched the old man. He swallowed and set down his plate, picked up his canteen, took a drink. He offered it to Bart, then set it down and picked up his plate again. "You stopped the bullets?"

"Not exactly, but that's the easiest way to describe it."

"How else would you describe it?" Cody broke off a piece of fish with the side of his fork.

Bart pursed his lips and raised his eyes, which glinted in the morning sun. "I controlled a force of nature that stopped the bullets. The Tatanka would say I *asked* nature to stop the bullets."

"It's magic." Cody smelled the fish on his fork before putting it into his mouth.

"That's another way to say it."

"Were you born with magic?"

Bart stared at the clouds for a long moment before answering. "We're all born with it, but it's a choice like everything else."

"Anyone could learn?"

"It's hard work."

"Someone could learn magic, like learning to make saddles or play the piano?"

Bart nodded. "I suppose it's like that."

Cody ate silently for a time. He watched Bart take the pan to the river, dunk it in the water, and scrub it with a cloth. Cody remembered the sound of the bullets slowing, then stopping – like the strongest wind he'd ever heard. He remembered seeing Grimshaw and Morgan on the plain. The thunder of Morgan's rifle and the smoke rising from the gun's barrel.

"Is the map gone for good?" he said. "Did I mess it all up?" He took a last bite and held out his plate to Bart.

"Messes can be cleaned," Bart said. "You can start with that plate." He tossed Cody the wet cloth. Cody frowned, but caught the rag and climbed to his feet. While he went to the river to wash the plate, Bart began to pack his equipment onto the dark bay mare.

Chapter 21

FEEL THE STONE, FEEL THE SKY

Cody and Bart rode west with the rising sun warm against their backs. Cody wondered what it would be like to control nature. He thought about the heat of the jail fire and the chilled air he felt as Bart extinguished the flames. The roaring wind that stalled the slugs from Morgan's rifle an arm's length from his chest. The tinkle and pulse of Mrs Ryder's piano, the way the sound surrounded and went through him, and the feelings it pulled from his heart.

Cody wondered how Mr and Mrs Ryder were doing, and if their baby had been born. Did they still think about him as he found himself thinking of them? They probably felt angry, he knew, but he liked that idea better than if they had already forgotten him. It felt like a long time since he had seen them. Everything that had happened since Pa shot the man on the coach felt so long ago. Cody wondered where Pa had gone. At each bend in the trail, he half expected to find his father waiting for him with a loaded gun in one hand and a whisky bottle in the other. He shook the thought from his mind and took a deep breath. He reached forwards and patted Smoke's neck.

The rocky trail was overgrown with tawny prairie grass and lined with broad swaths of it. Bart said no one used the road anymore since they built a bigger, smoother one a few years back. They both led to Fortune City, King's town, home to the Skyscraper, entryway to the Scar Mountains, and the place where they were heading. This road would get them there just as well, Bart said, and they'd less likely be noticed.

They topped a small rise and saw four buffalo grazing up ahead, their wooly hunched backs drifting like brown clouds over the tawny field. Near by, a stream of camp-fire smoke curled into the blue sky from the middle of a wooded hollow.

Bart and Cody dismounted and entered the woods. They found the three Tatanka warriors sitting around a low fire, a jackrabbit on a spit cooking in the heat. They stared at Cody as if he were a strange creature. The tall warrior scowled. Cody felt his heart rate rise but tried not to show it. He scanned the group and looked each man in the eyes. With their war paint gone, they looked more like men and less like deadly foes. Cody breathed.

The silver-haired warrior smiled. "Come. Sit," he said, patting the dirt.

Cody lowered himself tentatively to the ground beside the man. Bart sat next to the small, wiry warrior. He spoke to the man in words Cody could not understand. The other warriors laughed at what he said, but the wiry man looked at Cody thoughtfully. He drew a small stone from a pouch in his lap, closed his eyes, placed the stone against his lips, and whispered strangely.

Bart leant towards the silver-haired warrior now and spoke quietly to him. The man regarded Cody and nodded solemnly. He reached forwards and turned the spit. Cody's stomach groaned at the smoky smell of the cooking meat. The man saw him eyeing the rabbit and grinned. He turned it once more, then took a knife from his belt, sliced a long strip of meat, and passed it to Cody.

After they had eaten, the warriors rose in unison as if it had been rehearsed. Bart also stood and strolled over to the dark bay mare. Cody followed. As he watched Bart lift his saddle onto the horse's back, the silver-haired warrior appeared carrying the *mochila*. He handed it to Cody.

"You go now," he said and walked away.

Cody inspected the *mochila* and found it had not even been opened.

"What's going on?" he said, turning to face Bart. "He just told me to leave."

Bart glanced at Cody. "I heard."

"You don't want me around?"

Bart reached under the mare's chest and buckled the saddle strap.

Cody's face tightened and his eyes narrowed. His lips curled in a snarl.

"It's dangerous," Bart said.

"My whole life is dangerous." Cody could feel anger simmering in his gut.

Bart looked at him calmly. "It's not your fight."

"It's yours?"

Bart shrugged. "It's just the right thing I ought to do."

"I lost the map," Cody said. The tangled knot in his stomach twisted. "Where do you suppose I ought to go?"

Bart said nothing.

"I thought you wanted me around. I thought you were gonna teach me somethin'."

Bart's green eyes glinting.

"You can't send me away now," Cody said, glaring at the old man. "I'm comin'."

Bart pulled the strap tight and shook the saddle to make sure it was secure. "Ok. Good."

"Ok, good?" Cody clenched his fists. He wanted to scream. Was that a test? Ok, good? Hadn't Cody already proved himself? He wanted to shake the old man. Instead, he turned and walked away. He found his saddle and hoisted it onto Smoke's back. The horse nickered softly and Cody patted its neck.

"You're the only one who doesn't want to get rid of me," he said.

As he tightened the saddle to the mustang's back, Cody noticed the wiry warrior picking through the woods, collecting tiny stones and putting them into a small sack. At one point, the warrior stopped and looked at Cody and grinned. Then he went back to his work.

Cody slipped the *mochila* over the horn of his saddle. Despite everything else, he felt a sense of accomplishment. Mr Ryder, he thought, would be pleased to see his creation in one piece. Cody didn't know if he would ever deliver the mail, but at least he had the *mochila*.

⚬⚬

The Tatanka rode in a cluster a short distance ahead of Cody and Bart, who rode side-by-side, but without speaking a word. They forded a small river lined with broad boxwood trees and climbed a valley settled with pine and occasional oaks. The sun blazed, but the riders stayed cool in the trees' shade.

At the top of a steep hill, the wiry warrior twisted round to face Cody and threw a stone at him. It stung his chest and bounced to the ground. The warrior turned and continued on without a word. Cody looked at Bart, who shrugged.

"What was that for?"

"I believe Sky Weaver wants you to feel the stone."

Just then another small rock stung his neck. Cody turned to glare at the warrior, but again he was gone.

"Yes," Bart said. "He definitely wants you to feel the stone."

Cody rubbed the sore spot just below his chin. He wondered if the warrior might be crazy.

As they rode on, the sun began to set and long

shadows stretched across the trail. Bart whistled from time to time. And Sky Weaver launched rocks at Cody from time to time. Eventually, the shadows spread and ripened into darkness so that only steel-grey moonlight revealed the world. Then the riders pulled up beside a small river to rest for the night.

Cody unsaddled Smoke and set out his bedroll, along with his pack, saddle and *mochila,* at the far end of the clearing. He watered the mustang and let it loose to eat. A group of white-flowered crab apple trees grew near by and Smoke went right to them and began devouring the fallen fruit. When Cody turned around, he found his things thrown into the bushes and the tall warrior sitting where his bedroll had been.

The warrior's dark stone eyes set narrow and angry, his mouth straight and thin. Cody recognized the face of someone looking for a fight. He felt the slightest tingle in his fingers. He became aware that Bart and the other warriors were watching him. He glanced at his things in the bushes and then looked back at the tall warrior's face. His first thought was to touch the handle of his Colt to make sure it was ready, but he held back from doing so. A thin tree bent and creaked in the breeze. The tall warrior grinned.

Sky Weaver stepped forwards then and collected Cody's things from the bushes. He handed the bedroll and packs to Cody and led him away, carrying the saddle himself.

"Bear Claw Man is young and likes to show he's a warrior," he said. "Put your things near mine. We have work to do."

Sky Weaver sat on a blanket, which was already spread out on the dirt. He stared up at the sky while Cody laid out his bedroll. When he was settled, Cody sat and followed Sky Weaver's gaze into the night. The stars hung like tiny golden points on a vast, black map.

"Bart says you wish to speak to Big Sky," Sky Weaver said without looking down. "To ask favours of the earth."

Cody lifted off his hat and set it on the dirt near his pack. "You can teach me?"

The warrior looked at him now and nodded. "You have learned the first step yourself," he said. "To want to know."

He took a small stone from the dirt and pinched it between his thumb and forefinger. He held it out to Cody, then snapped it at his cheek.

"You have learned the second lesson," he said. "To feel the stone."

"That was a lesson?" Cody said, rubbing the sting out of his skin.

Sky Weaver smiled. "To feel the stone," he repeated.

"What's the third lesson?" Cody asked.

"To feel the sky."

Cody wasn't sure how he was going to do that. He wasn't even sure what it meant.

CHAPTER 22

SPEAKING TO BIG SKY

When Sky Weaver woke Cody, pale moonlight still clung to the sky. The boy crawled from under his blanket while the others still slept. The bracing chill brought him quickly awake and he opened his mouth to ask what they were doing, but Sky Weaver shook his head. He reached for his boots, but again Sky Weaver shook his head.

"Come," he said with the slightest gesture of his fingers.

Cody followed the Tatanka downstream, the bottoms of his feet stung by the cold, rocky ground. They stopped at a slow elbow in the river where, without a word of explanation, Sky Weaver turned and waded backwards into the water, watching Cody intently as he stepped.

Cody, in return, studied the man. He looked younger than Bart, maybe Pa's age, and his earthy skin stretched smoothly across his frame except where two jagged scars puckered his chest. His face, too, was unsmooth, having wrinkles and roughness from the wind and sun. Two bright blue feathers tangled within his long, black hair.

"Come," he said, motioning Cody forwards.

Cody stepped into the chill water and felt himself suddenly shivering. He sloshed deeper, arms wrapped tightly to his chest.

Sky Weaver held a small stone in his hand. He raised it high, and Cody flinched, thinking he meant to throw it. Instead, the Tatanka laughed and dropped the stone into the water.

"The ripples move outwards from the stone," he said.

Cody waited for more. He already knew a stone made ripples. He wasn't dumb. But Sky Weaver said nothing more. He only stared at Cody. Then he led him upstream until they stood between the pool and a mild stretch of rapids above. Sky Weaver sunk his hands into the water, and Cody copied him. He looked at Cody, his dark eyes glinted. "Feel the current," he said. "When you can feel the sky, it is like the current."

Cody pressed with his palms against the rushing

water. He felt the current pushing against them. He could feel it, but he'd never felt the sky that way. He'd felt the wind, but he didn't think that was what Sky Weaver meant.

"When you learn to speak to Big Sky, you can push the sky like the rock pushes the ripples of water."

Sky Weaver spread his arms and fell back into the river. The current pulled him under and his form blurred like a silty cloud stirred from the river bottom. His body drifted slowly down-current below the surface until it reached the pool and floated back upwards, his chest and face peeking from the water like small, dark islands. "It can push you or hold you. Or take you under." He disappeared beneath the water and reappeared a moment later by the shore. "So you must learn to swim."

⌒⌒

Cody rode beside Sky Weaver as the group headed for Fortune City. The land shifted alternately from broad prairies to pine and spruce valleys before finally turning to coarse, flat plains. Cody watched the buffalo ridden by the Tatanka, amazed at how they rumbled, even at a walk. The beasts grunted and bellowed constantly, and smelled rank in the heat. He watched Bart and the old warrior, who rode side-by-side and spoke ceaselessly, sometimes with words Cody understood, sometimes with words he did not. They laughed often and heartily.

Bear Claw Man rode stiffly and grim-faced. When he noticed Cody watching, his lips curled in a snarl and he snapped his gaze towards the boy, eyes wide and wild. Cody's own eyes snapped forwards. He patted Smoke's neck and stared straight ahead, risking only brief furtive glances, until Bear Claw Man finally looked away.

Cody thought for a time about the three Tatanka he now travelled with, how they each seemed so different. Pa would say Cody had joined a pack of bloodthirsty savages, and that he would end up on the point of a spear if he didn't watch his back. Cody feared that could be true with Bear Claw Man, but he didn't feel the same about the other two warriors. Could they each be so different? Could he be so different from Pa? He turned to Sky Weaver, who still rode beside him.

"Have you always ridden together?" he said, gesturing subtly towards the other Tatanka. "You seem so different."

Sky Weaver looked at Cody curiously, but not with displeasure. "Every man is different. These are my tribe, but I have travelled with many tribes in seeking Big Sky."

"But you came back to your own folks?" Cody said.

"Did you learn everything about Big Sky?"

Sky Weaver smiled and shook his head. "I have seen many trees and mountains, and sailed on oceans, and visited places where it never thaws. I have seen strange beasts and strange customs. But no one can know all of Big Sky."

"So why did you come back?"

"I was needed – to help find the map."

"To El Dorado?"

"The vaquero call it that, but we have no name for it."

Cody found it strange that they could have a city of gold and not even name it.

Sky Weaver pointed towards the silver-haired warrior. "Map Dreamer searches for the map. I help him."

"Why him?" Cody asked.

"The map was lost many seasons ago, before Map Dreamer's grandfather's grandfather was born. Men find the map and follow it to our home. They look for gold."

"White men?" Cody said.

"White men and dark men. It matters not. When they come, the Tatanka fight these men to protect our home. But when Map Dreamer was your age, he had a vision that it would be better to find the map than to fight.

"Map Dreamer told his vision to the chief and tribal elders. They laughed and said the world was too big to find one small map. But Map Dreamer didn't care. He set out before the sun rose again." Sky Weaver sighed and frowned. "He has not been home since."

"Does he know magic like you?"

"He speaks to Big Sky, but not in the same way."

"I don't think I'll ever feel the sky like you do."

"It may take many seasons. First you must work. With work, you will find small successes. Then you will believe. Only when you believe, can you feel the sky." Sky Weaver leant towards Cody and held out a pebble in his open palm. "Practice with this stone," he said. "Feel the sky around it. Cradle the stone in sky and lift it."

The stone rose up from Sky Weaver's hand and hovered there until Cody reached out and curled his fingers around it.

⌒~⌒

They rode on for two more days. A sudden shower one afternoon left the buffalo stinking, but the trip was otherwise uneventful. Now and again, Sky Weaver whipped small stones at Cody.

"Some day," he said, "you will stop the stones. For now, feel them." Then he laughed and Cody decided that Sky Weaver just enjoyed hearing him yelp.

Still, Cody held the stone in his hand as they rode. Stared at it resting in his palm. Closed his eyes and squeezed it. Tried to feel the sky around it.

But it felt like a rock.

At one frustrating moment, he threw it down on the trail. Then he leapt from his saddle and crawled in the dirt on his hands and knees to find it. Smoke, meanwhile, continued on and Cody had to chase him down and climb into the saddle as the mustang plodded ahead.

"I could do without the lesson," he said.

He nudged the horse ahead and pulled alongside Bart. "I can't do this," he said. "Tell me how to do it."

Bart regarded Cody and smiled. "No one can tell you how to feel the sky. You'll have to work that out."

"Sky Weaver told me," Cody said. "I just want you to explain it again."

Bart's bright green eyes glinted. "Sky Weaver told you what the sky feels like, not how to feel it."

Cody felt his face tighten in a scowl. "So you tell me."

"Wouldn't do any good if I did," Bart said. "You have to try for yourself."

"I've been staring at this stone for two days."

"That's a start."

Late on the third afternoon, the whole of Fortune City came into view across a vast expanse of dirt and scrub grass. At the outer edges, rows of small white houses stood in long neat rows. Beyond those wood structures stood rows of larger brick buildings. And then the Skyscraper. And then the mountains.

The group stopped, and Bart spoke to Map Dreamer in words Cody didn't understand. The old warrior responded, and then Bart set off towards the town.

"Come along, Cody," he called over his shoulder.

Cody looked at Sky Weaver, who gestured with a flick of his head that Cody should go.

"We can't go into town," he said, "but we'll be there when we're needed. Be careful, and keep searching for Big Sky." He held up a hand to Cody.

Cody waved and set his heels to Smoke's flanks. The two set off after Bart on the road to Fortune City.

Chapter 23

FORTUNE CITY

The Scar Mountains tore out of the Freelands like rows of jagged teeth straining to devour the sky. Dark stone ascents mottled with pine and aspen, sharp peaks capped with pale snow, the mountains surged and dipped in violent waves like the rapids of a swollen river, a barricade between East and West. But in one narrow span, the angry rock plunged steeply to a cut, a dark, winding valley that men and wagons could negotiate with effort, a lone passage to the west.

At the foot of this cut stood the Skyscraper, a towering rise of grey stone blocks, blank and impenetrable, enclosing some secret, dangerous interior. The mountain's severe ridges hovered behind it like fiendish, serrated wings. Light could enter the structure only through the rows of dark windows that bisected the upper reaches like watchful, menacing eyes. Men could enter only at the structure's base where a broad opening stretched, thick with darkness that seemed to swallow the light.

Fortune City poured from the shadow of the brooding tower. Brick and wood buildings lined the wide main road that disappeared into the Skyscraper's dark maw. Along Main Street, Cody noted a bank, a general store, a barber shop, a telegraph office, a theatre, a coach company, a boarding stable, two hotels and three saloons. Clusters of men stood beside doorways, talking and watching passers-by. Men and women flitted in and out of shops. A newspaper boy called out the day's headlines.

The bank stood nearest the Skyscraper, windowless and brick, with walls enclosing its flat rooftop. A man with a rifle patrolled the rooftop and watched the street outside the bank's entrance.

Cody and Bart walked the crowded street, leading Smoke and the dark bay mare. Large ox-drawn wagons emerged in small groups from the Skyscraper's dim mouth and followed the road east. Smaller, mule-drawn wagons exited the back and followed the road west into the mountains.

Cody watched a man stumble through the split half-doors of one saloon and tumble into the street. He climbed to his feet, dusted the front of his shirt, grumbling, and staggered to another saloon down the road.

A memory of Pa started to form in Cody's mind when he felt a small rock sting the back of his head. He turned to find Bart grinning at him, his green eyes sparkling.

Cody scowled. "I don't see how that helps."

Bart shrugged.

"How am I supposed to feel a rock before it hits me?" Cody had been trying to raise the stone from his palm all day, but he felt no magic; he felt nothing but a stone sitting in his hand.

"Maybe you can't," Bart said.

"But you do it."

"Then maybe you can." Bart stopped and scanned the road, then looked back at Cody. "But truly you can't."

Cody exhaled sharply and glared.

"By the time you feel the stone, it's too late." Bart grinned and Cody's jaw tightened. "The trick," he said, "is to feel the ripples from the stone."

Bart set off again and Cody followed, thinking of Sky Weaver's lesson in the river. Shortly, they stopped in front of the Good Fortune Hotel, a white, wooden building with a second-story balcony that stretched its length. On the ground floor a large square window exposed a dining room where two waitresses moved about busily serving well-dressed diners.

"Let's tie the horses here," Bart said, wrapping the dark bay's lead around a post.

Cody patted the mustang's neck. "I don't need to tie Smoke." The horse responded with a low snort.

Bart nodded, walked forwards, and pulled open the double doors that led into the hotel. Cody patted Smoke's neck once more, then followed Bart inside.

When he stepped into the hotel lobby, part of Cody felt like sneaking back out, like it was too fine a place for him to enter, but another part of him wanted to spit on the polished wood floors, which looked overly fine for anyone's needs. Walls of dark wood met white beamed ceilings where icy chandeliers hung, glinting with their own light. A clerk stood behind a long, smooth wooden desk. He wore a pinstriped shirt and a dark-blue vest. He reminded Cody of Mr Waddell from the Express.

Bart walked to the desk and requested a room. The clerk examined his log book and scratched several notes. Bart reached in his pocket and drew out a gold coin, which he placed on the desk. The clerk's eyes widened a hint when he looked at the coin, and his mouth turned up in a greedy grin. He took the coin and stepped through a doorway behind the desk. He returned a moment later and handed Bart a key.

Cody and Bart sat in the dining room eating steak, baked potatoes and carrots. The plates were shining and white and reflected an image of the chandelier overhead. Cody had never eaten in a restaurant other than a saloon. He felt strange when the waitress took their order and delivered their food and asked if he needed anything else. It felt different from when Mrs Ryder filled his plate or asked him what he needed. This didn't feel quite right to him. Still, the cooking tasted nearly as good as Mrs Ryder's and Cody devoured everything on his plate. When he finally looked up, he noticed that Bart's food lay mostly untouched. The old man stared out the window, his eyes scanning the people who passed.

"What are you lookin' for?" Cody said.

"Not sure. Just wondering how we ought to get King's attention."

"Why would we do that?" Cody asked.

But Bart didn't answer. He stood, never turning his gaze from the window, and put on his hat. "Speak of the devil," he said. "Come on, son."

Bart led Cody down the street, where a crowd gathered in front of the Four Aces Saloon, a sturdy wooden box with smoke-stained windows. The people held strangely quiet, only the stomp and grunt of oxen and the roll of wooden wheels over the packed dirt road could be heard. Bart grabbed Cody's arm and pulled him into the crowd. "Stay close," he said, pushing his way through the people until they emerged at the front of the throng.

A black man in a fine grey suit and rattlesnake boots lay on the ground, his mouth swollen and bleeding. He propped himself on an elbow and wiped the blood from his lips with the back of his hand. He stared with practised neutrality at a slight, dark haired man standing over him.

The man's blue eyes scanned the crowd then returned to the man lying at his boots. He set his angular face sternly, his eyes ablaze with disdain. He tugged at the wrists of his black leather gloves. He smoothed the front of his black shirt with the palm of one gloved hand. He moved a strand of hair from his forehead. He watched the fallen man silently, seeming to dare him to move or even speak. Behind him stood a gang of hired guns; Cody could tell by the way they glowered at the fallen man. Beside him stood Gus Grimshaw, long coat draped behind his holster, fingertips brushing the butt of his revolver. The crowd held perfectly silent. A crow cawed.

Cody felt a tingle build in his fingers when he recognized Grimshaw. He glanced at the saloon's rooftop looking for Morgan. He looked at Bart nervously.

The old man winked. "They can't see us," he whispered.

Cody remembered the sheriff looking through them outside the charred jailhouse. The tingle stayed in his fingers went no further.

Finally, the gloved man spoke, his voice cold and even, edged like a knife blade. The lack of emotion in his voice chilled Cody. "You've been gambling away money you owe me." Grimshaw glanced at the man, waiting on a command, and Cody realized the man was King.

The gambler shook his head. "That ain't so." He pushed himself off the ground and rested his weight on one knee. "I'll get your money quick."

"Is that right?" King said. He smiled grimly. "Is it in your pocket?"

The gambler shook his head. His eyes lost their practiced cool.

King held out a gloved hand. "Is it in the bank? Because I'll hoist you up myself and we can walk down together and make a withdrawal."

The man's eyes, now wide with alarm, moved pleadingly over the crowd then fell to the ground. "No," he said quietly. "but I've got family."

"Family with the money you owe me?"

"No," the man said, looking back at King. "But I want to see them."

King tugged at his gloves again.

"I'll get your money."

"If this were last week," King said, "that would have helped us both. Now get up."

The gambler's jaw tightened and quivered. He climbed to his feet and straightened his back. He closed his eyes and inhaled deeply. Then he opened his eyes and the alarm was gone from them. He neatened his jacket and waited for King to act.

The silence was so severe, Cody could hear the gambler breathing. He could hear the flutter of a bird's wings overhead. He could hear the thud of his own heart.

Finally, King gave the slightest nod, almost imperceptible.

Grimshaw drew his pistol and fired a single shot. The splatter of blood from the gambler's head appeared instantaneously, as if there were no bullet and the sound alone had inflicted the damage. The man's legs crumpled and he half slumped, half fell to the road. His head bounced once off the hard ground with a thud, then settled in the dirt. His eyes, still open and staring towards Cody, showed no alarm.

Cody closed his own eyes and inhaled the burnt gunpowder smell. A shudder leapt through his body.

"Bill, drag this unreliable corpse out to Blood Hill and dig him a hole," King said. "Jessup can help."

Cody's eyes shot open. The tingle in his fingers rushed through his limbs and into his chest as Pa pushed his way through King's gang of hired guns. His sneering gaze swept over the crowd as he stomped towards the dead man and looked straight at Cody. His long nose twitched, and the knot in Cody's stomach uncoiled like a rattlesnake. Cody held his breath, certain that Pa could see him or smell him. Finally, Pa turned and reached down and grabbed the dead man by his boots. He lifted the lifeless legs and waited for his partner to lift the other half of the body.

A black feather floated through a remnant of gun smoke. With a slight shift of the breeze, it drifted towards Cody. He felt its ripple just before it landed. He watched it touch down and come to rest on his shoulder. He felt its weight.

Chapter 24

A Sleepless Night

Bart placed a hand on Cody's back and led him away from the Four Aces Saloon. Cody's head felt cloudy, as if he had held his breath too long. His limbs felt numb and buoyed, and the sound of his boots scuffing the dirt road did not connect in his mind with his footsteps. An image of the falling Okwaho warrior flashed in his mind, a spray of crimson, the smoke from Cody's revolver curling into the sky. Then Pa grabbing the dead gambler by his boots, the snakeskin tips angling awkwardly from the crooks of his arms. Cody shook his head trying to cast away the images. He closed and then opened his eyes and they focused on the world once more. He watched King and his gang saunter up the road towards the Skyscraper. The shopkeepers who had watched the murder from the doorways of their shops shuffled back inside as King's gang passed.

Outside the Good Fortune Hotel, Cody stopped. Something felt wrong, something besides all the obviously wrong things. He touched a fingertip to the Colt at his waist. He felt Bart's hand still resting against his back. He slowly scanned the road from the Skyscraper to the edge of town. Finally he settled his attention nearer. Something was missing. The dark bay mare stood calmly tied to a post outside the hotel. Smoke had been standing beside the mare when Cody and Bart headed towards the Four Aces. Now the mare stood alone. And while Cody knew that the mustang might head off for a run or to graze, he also knew that wasn't the case this time.

"Smoke's gone. He always knows when there's gonna be trouble."

Bart nodded. "Come on. Let's get some rest."

They climbed the stairs to the hotel's second floor and found the room that matched the number on Bart's key. Bart opened the door and stepped inside with Cody following behind. He went to the window and drew shut the white lace curtains. Cody stopped just through the doorway and took stock of the room, which held two narrow brass beds, a smooth walnut dresser, and a matching nightstand between the beds. A clear glass oil lamp stood on the nightstand and Cody felt drawn to it, as if were a familiar object, as if he had expected it to be there. Something about the lamp made the room more inviting to him. He stared at the shining glass and the flame, which glowed dimly in the shadowy room. He tried to feel the small fire's heat on his cheek as he had felt the feather's weight on his shoulder. He thought of the ripples in the water and of the jailhouse fire, how it had started with the flame of one small match. He tried to feel the lamp's heat ripple outwards and touch his cheek.

"Son," Bart said, "you ought to crawl into one of these beds and get some rest. It's been a tough stretch."

Cody reached back and shut the door. He took off his hat and set it on the floor. He stripped down to his underclothes and climbed into the bed. He pulled the blankets up to his chin. The day was warm and sunny, but Cody felt chilled. The bed was comfortable, but he didn't feel like he could sleep. He closed his eyes and listened to the creak of springs as Bart climbed into the other bed.

Pa's small, dark eyes flashed in Cody's mind and his own eyes sprung open. He shook his head and took a deep breath. His heart beat rapidly. He stared up at the white ceiling.

"Bart?" he said. "How'd you make them not see us? Pa looked straight at me."

"I didn't make them not see us," Bart said. "I just made us not seen."

Cody looked over at the old man who lay on his back, hands behind his head, eyes closed. "You know what I mean," he said. "It's the same thing."

"It is not the same thing," Bart said, glancing sideways at Cody with squinted eyes. "You need to learn to recognize such differences."

"Fine," Cody said. He wasn't exactly sure what the old man meant, and he didn't feel like he cared. He just wished Bart would answer a question directly for once. But he had no energy to argue about it now. "Then how did you make us not seen?" he said. "It wasn't the wind. Like with the bullets."

"Light," Bart said, closing his eyes again. "You can't see anything in the dark, can you?"

"I can't," Cody answered.

"So if the light doesn't touch you, nobody ought to be able to see you. Right?"

Cody grunted vaguely. He truthfully didn't know

why you couldn't see in the dark.

"The Tatanka would say that I asked the light not to touch us."

Cody held his hand towards the lamp and tried to imagine the orange glow bending around his fingers.

"The light carries what we see like the breeze carries what we smell."

Cody remembered Pa staring at him, the twitch of his hawkish nose. "I guess you didn't talk to the breeze," he said, "because I'm pretty sure Pa smelt me."

Bart laughed and Cody laughed too. Some tension eased from Cody's body and he became aware of the pillow's softness beneath his head. He closed his eyes and let sleep overtake him.

⟲⟳

When he woke, the lamp was dark and a curtain of black sky hung outside the windows. Cody's heart raced. Beads of sweat clung to his forehead and his chest felt clammy. Though he recalled no details of it, he knew he had been having a nightmare. He felt his mind searching for the memory, so he tried to focus on other things. Bart's slow rasping breaths. Crickets chirping. Drunks calling to one another in the street. He threw off his covers and sat up on the edge of the bed. He thought to reach across and rouse Bart, but decided to let the old man sleep.

Instead, he rose and walked to the window. He moved aside the curtain and observed a sliver of moon hanging over the mountains. He tried not to look at the Skyscraper but it dominated the sky. He raised the window and climbed through the opening onto the balcony.

Standing there in his underclothes in the dim light and the cool breeze, Cody felt the breath return to his lungs. He inhaled deeply and rubbed his chest over his heart. The boards beneath his feet creaked. He sighed. He wondered how he got involved in such a mess. Did it start when Pa abandoned him at the jail or when Bart rescued him from the flames? Maybe it started when he met the Ryders or when he signed on with the Express. Maybe it started with Smoke. Cody couldn't say for sure, but he could not go where this was leading. Not after he had seen King in action. Not after he had seen Pa working for King. He had travelled so far to get away from Pa, and here he was again. Cody knew now, without doubt, that he didn't want to live with Pa ever again. He didn't want to tangle with Pa ever again.

Cody heard footsteps and turned to find Bart approaching. The old man crouched down so his face was at the window's opening just above the sill. He smiled at Cody, then looked past him towards the Skyscraper.

"King don't seem like one to cross," Cody said. He followed Bart's gaze. Shadows stretched and coiled like snakes around the building's stone walls.

"I suppose not," Bart said.

"And I know Pa ain't," Cody said. "I done it before and I'd rather not make it a habit."

He looked at Bart. He could tell the old man knew what he was thinking. He expected Bart to look angry, but he didn't. He looked calm as usual, except his white hair was mussed about the bald top of his head. His green eyes sparkled.

"You don't have to do this," Bart said finally. "It's not your fight."

Cody looked at the moon. He felt both relieved and ashamed. He wished he could keep the moonlight off himself so he couldn't be seen. He had nothing to do with El Dorado, Cody told himself. He just found a map. The Tatanka had warriors who could fight King. He was just a boy.

And he didn't want to have to kill anyone else. Ever. Even if they deserved it.

Cody looked back towards the window, but Bart was already gone.

He didn't know what he planned to say anyway.

Cody stepped forwards and set his hands on the balcony's railing. He looked down to the road in front of the hotel to see if Smoke was there, though he knew before he looked that the horse had not returned. He sighed and gazed down the main street of Fortune City. The shops stood quietly except for the saloons, which buzzed and shook. Cody watched the door of the Four Aces, half expecting Pa to stumble out. He wondered if that's want he would do when he grew older, stumble in and out of saloons, fighting and gambling. He thought about the dead man who had gambled away the money he owed King. Did that man have a family like Pa did, and would they be better off without him?

Cody wished he had died with his mother. Then they'd be together and he wouldn't have to decide where to go now. He lay down on the balcony. If he couldn't sleep, at least he could rest in the cool air. The jangle and ting of a piano reached his ears just as his mind began to quiet. The sound was faint, but Cody could make out a melody interspersed with the calls of drunken men. For a time he listened, trying to hum along with the tune. He thought about playing the piano with Mrs Ryder, her thin brown fingers moving over the glossy white keys, the warmth and softness of her body sitting beside him, her smile and the feeling of the music surrounding him and pouring out of him.

Then Cody remembered the sack of gold inside the piano and his hand reaching into it. The stolen coins still weighed down his trouser pocket. He hoped someday to return them unspent. He hoped they would forgive him.

The breeze blew and carried the scent of a distant flower. Cody inhaled deeply and found himself thinking about the El Dorado map. He had to admit to himself that, like the coins, he had stolen the map. Bart and the Tatanka would have it now if he had not taken it from the strongbox during the stagecoach robbery. He was responsible for the lost map, just as he was responsible for the stolen coins in his pocket.

Cody knew the Tatanka had families like the Ryders, mothers and fathers and children. They had homes. He wondered if they played music like Mrs Ryder. He hoped they did.

Once again, Cody knew what he had to do. But this time it didn't feel wrong. This time he didn't feel ashamed. The fact that Pa was involved only made it more clear. Just as he felt responsible for the lost map and the coins in his pocket, he somehow felt responsible for whatever misfortune Pa might bring to the situation.

Cody stood up and climbed through the window. He saw a glint of Bart's green eyes and knew the old man was still awake.

"Do you think Smoke will come back?" he said.

"I imagine he will," Bart said. "Now get some sleep. We have important work to do tomorrow."

Chapter 25

BLOOD HILL

Cody carried a load of old shotguns and rifles up the front side of Blood Hill. The guns, black and bent and heavy, were piled high and awkwardly in the crooks of his outstretched arms. His feet slipped on the damp leafy weeds that covered the ground, which was pocked with loose dirt mounds where the dead had been buried. A few of the graves were marked with crosses or inscribed wood scraps jammed into the dirt, but most lay unremembered. Cody thought by the putrid smell and the frenzy of insects crawling and flying over some of the mounds that the holes had not been dug deeply enough. He tried not to breathe, but it only caused him to take fewer, deeper breaths of the noxious air as he laboured up the hill. He coughed from the stench and jerked his head randomly to keep the flies and gnats off his face.

The top of the hill levelled off and Cody found Bart standing under a lone oak tree. Half of the tree's upper reaches had been cleaved off by lightning or wind long ago, and the resulting cleft gave the tree the appearance of a claw sticking out of the earth. The ground here was more settled, as if the dead had come to terms with their demise. The mounds were sunken and covered with patches of weeds and scrub grass. In a number of places, clumps of thick bushes grew. Cody opened his arms and let the guns tumble down against the oak's trunk. He shook out his tired limbs and wiped his face to erase the sweat and the lingering itch of insect bites. Bart glanced at the weapons but didn't say anything. Then he turned towards the road, which wound around the steep embankment on the back side of Blood Hill and stretched far eastwards into the horizon.

A short distance ahead, two ox-drawn wagons rode away from Fortune City carrying goods to sell in the eastern territories. Farther out, just barely visible, a passenger coach drawn by a team of four horses followed the road west.

"That's the one," Bart said.

"The one what?" Cody asked. He had carried the

guns without complaint or question, because he trusted Bart, and because he had guessed they were heading out to meet the Tatanka. He welcomed the chance to talk with Sky Weaver again. Now, with three rifles and four shotguns massed under the tree, and Bart eyeing an approaching stagecoach, Cody felt uneasy. He could vaguely hear Bart responding, but the words failed to register any meaning.

He thought back to the day that had started his journey across the Freelands, the stagecoach hold-up and the bald man whose blood spread across his white shirt like a ripple spreading through the water. The women's screams. The chase and the hoof beats. Gunshots and the paint mare falling. Jail and Pa's sneer in the barred window. A match falling. Flame.

Cody found himself pacing along the edge of the embankment, staring down at the worn, but well-groomed, dirt road. His jaw and his chest felt tight. His mind grew thick with a tangle of things he might say. He lifted off his grey hat with one hand and dragged the fingers of his other hand through his hair.

"You mean to hold up that stagecoach, don't you?"

Bart's movements seemed to slow then. His glimmering green eyes held a hint of surprise. "That's the aim." He spoke with a lack of certainty that was unusual for the old man.

Cody glanced at the weapons lying at the base of the tree. He shook his head. The tightness in his muscles pulsed. The thickness in his mind turned and twisted. Sadness. Fear. Confusion. Anger.

"You're no better than him!"

The surprise in Bart's eyes grew.

"You expect me to shoot who's in that coach? Or watch you do it?" Cody was shouting. His face was taut and red. He stepped towards Bart. Though he was barely aware of it, his fingers touched the handle of his Colt.

Bart took a step back. "Slow down, son. You've got it wrong."

"Don't call me son," Cody said. The words erupted from his mouth, spit flying from his lips. His fingers curled around the handle of his Colt. With his other hand, he shoved Bart in the chest. The old man stumbled backwards. His heel slipped on the edge of the embankment. He fell from the edge, his arms shooting up and out to the sides as if he were being held at gunpoint. His black bowler hat tumbled into the air. He landed on his back with a thud. A hard, unexpected breath escaped his lungs.

Now Cody's gun was drawn and he glared down at the old man lying in the dirt below him. "You want me to be like him?" His voice strained with rage.

Bart shook his head, not lifting it from the dirt. "No," he said, barely audible.

Cody kicked a fist-sized rock and it hurtled down to the road and slammed into the dirt an arm's length from Bart's head. The old man watched the rock's path, twisting his body away from the impact, then easing himself back flat against the road.

Almost unaware, Cody stretched his arm forwards until the Colt aimed at the old man's chest. "I'm not like Pa," he said. His words echoed in his own ears, as if they were spoken by a distant stranger. "I won't be like Pa."

Bart nodded slowly. "Then put away that gun."

Cody looked down at the weapon in his hand. His forearm was chiselled with strain, his fingers and knuckles red. He didn't feel his hand at all. He looked down at Bart, still lying in the road. The old man's face looked calm and neutral, but his eyes still held a hint of surprise.

"What would your pa do?" Bart said.

Cody felt the question like the sting of a bee, just enough pain to wake him. He knew that in this situation

Pa wouldn't have let Bart speak so many words. He'd have plugged the old man by now. But that wasn't how Cody wanted to be. He let his arm relax and his fist unclench. He lowered the Colt and replaced it in its holster.

Bart smiled. "Now let me tell you the plan," he said. "You need to trust me."

Cody knew Pa wouldn't trust the old man. He had never trusted anyone.

The rock lay beside Bart's head, heavy enough to have cracked his skull. Cody wasn't certain whether or not he had meant for it to strike Bart. He only knew he kicked it at him. Now he stared at it. Now he felt its weight.

Chapter 26

HOLD UP

Bart stood in the road as the stagecoach approached. He wore no bandana to hide his face and held no gun. He extended his arm, palm out, to the oncoming coach.

The driver, a broad, thick-gutted man, called out harshly and snapped the reins to his four black horses. Beside him sat a thinner, square-shouldered guard, who raised a shotgun to his shoulder. The coach sped forwards, quickly closing on Bart.

Cody watched from the top of Blood Hill, crouched behind a scraggly juniper. He held a shotgun, which he gripped tightly as the coach drove towards Bart, a wake of dust rising from its wheels.

Bart spoke a strange word and his green eyes glinted.

Cody felt a pulse. A silence. A shiver in the air.

The four black horses suddenly reared up, their back hooves digging into the road, dragging the stagecoach to an abrupt stop. The driver and guard lurched forwards in their seats. The driver's rumpled tan hat flopped from his head, dropped between the horses, and landed on the dirt where the frightened team stomped it with their hooves. The guard's shotgun slammed down against the frame of the coach with a crack.

The two coachmen jerked themselves upright in their seats. Cody expected Bart to somehow disarm the guard, but he didn't. Instead, he dropped his arms casually to his sides. In his black trousers and jacket and his matching bowler, he looked like a banker awaiting his next client.

"How'd you stop them horses?" the driver said.

"Shut it, Earl," the guard snapped. His narrow-set eyes held a cold, hawkish look. He repositioned the shotgun at his shoulder and drew back both hammers with a single sweep of his thumb. He motioned with the barrel of his gun towards the side of the road. "Get out of the way, old man."

"I can do that," Bart said. "After you give me the strongbox." He nodded his head casually, as if he and the man were negotiating a business deal.

The man's hands and forearms tensed and he leant his head sideways towards the barrel of the gun.

"You ought not do that," Bart said. He pointed casually towards the top of Blood Hill. "My partners wouldn't appreciate it."

The coachmen's eyes darted up the embankment where Bart and Cody had set the three rifles and three of the shotguns pointing from the bushes towards the road. The guns were balanced on sticks and rocks. Cody held the fourth shotgun, similarly aimed towards the coach. Now he raised the barrel upward and pulled off a shot. The blast echoed across the plain. The horses whinnied and stomped nervously.

"Whoa," the driver called to the team, drawing slack from the reins.

Cody set down the gun and crawled to the next weapon in the row, a rifle. He kneeled and lifted the butt to his shoulder. He shifted his aim so the coachmen could see the barrel moving.

"Old man, you're making a mistake," the guard said. "The gold we're hauling belongs to Tyrus King."

"Wouldn't be worth as much if it didn't," Bart said.

The man looked at him suspiciously for a time, then spat. "Aright," he said with a shake of his head. "But you're gonna find yourself looking at Blood Hill from beneath the dirt." He lowered the barrel of his gun and slowly reset the hammers.

Bart approached the coach and extended his arm towards the guard, who handed him the gun. Bart snapped it open and removed the shells. Then he tossed them, along with the weapon, to the side of the road.

"Climb on down," he said. He looked across at the driver. "You too. And give me the revolvers from your holsters."

Bart collected three six-shooters from the two coachmen. He smiled at them as he took the guns from their hands. He opened the cylinder of each one and removed the bullets. Then he tossed the ammunition and guns to the side of the road.

"We don't want anyone to get hurt," he said, grinning.

As all this happened, Cody trained his rifle on the coachmen. He felt strangely aware that he experienced no tingle in his fingers. No buzz in his chest. No snakes in his stomach. He never worried that Bart would be hurt. He never worried that he'd need to fire a shot at the coachmen.

"Any passengers?" Bart said.

The driver looked to the guard, who offered a nod.

"Come on out," Bart said. "Slow and smart and easy, and you'll be fine."

The door opened, and a man emerged with his hands raised. He wore a black suit and bowler hat. His hair and moustache were thick and brown. He looked to Cody like a younger version of Bart. "Come on," the man said, leaning in towards the opening and nodding encouragingly. A boy of eight or nine years stepped cautiously from the coach, his arms raised high as if he meant to reach something on a shelf above his head. His eyes were wide and glassy. His arms shook.

"Good boy," the man said. "Nobody means us any harm. Isn't that right, mister?"

Bart tipped his hat and smiled. His green eyes glinted, and the boy grinned. "That's certainly right. Go ahead and lower your arms," he said. "Any revolvers?"

"Left it in the coach," the boy's father said.

Bart nodded approvingly. The two men exchanged an agreeable look.

"I'm gonna tie you all," Bart said. "But we'll send someone from town to fetch you." He looked at the boy and winked. "So don't worry none."

He herded the three men and the boy around the side of Blood Hill. "Cody," he called. "Come on out and give me a hand."

Cody climbed to his feet and walked along the top of the hill above Bart and the captives until they reached a place where the embankment eased into the hillside. Then they climbed the hill towards Cody, who backed slowly away and kept his rifle aimed at the coachmen. When the guard crested the hill, his face turned red and his fists and jaw clenched tightly. He leant forwards as if he meant to charge. Cody set his aim and glanced at Bart.

"We got no reason," Bart said, "to tell anyone you surrendered to an unarmed old man and a boy with a rifle."

Cody turned and saw that the unmanned guns propped in the bushes were plainly visible now.

The guard shook his head and exhaled sharply. He still looked angry but smiled a little. "Other men fall for that?"

"Plenty," Bart said. "And usually without my partner, who made it all much more convincing." Bart winked at Cody, who felt a pleasant sensation like when Mr Ryder had admired his leather work.

The guard half laughed and half growled. He couldn't seem to decide how to respond to the trick that had been played on him. The driver, for his part, looked mildly confused.

Cody looked at the young boy, who stared at his rifle as if it were a coiled rattler. He could feel the weight of the boy's fear. He tried to curl his lips into a smile, but the boy's expression didn't change. Instead, he turned and hugged his father's leg.

Bart tied the three men and the boy in the shade of the oak tree, and gave each one a drink of water from a canteen. He stuffed a note in the guard's pocket.

"A message for Mr King," he said.

Chapter 27

OUTLAW

Cody and Bart hobbled down the dirt road, one on each side of the heavy wooden strongbox, gripping sturdy leather handles attached to each end. Not far from Blood Hill, they stopped where a solitary boulder stood a dozen steps from the road. "Let's bury this here," Bart said, "behind the rock."

"Ain't we gonna open it?" Cody said.

"It's gold," Bart said. "You seen gold before?"

Cody nodded.

"Then no need to open it."

Cody felt anger stir inside himself. He didn't appreciate Bart's curt reply, but even more, some part of him desired to open the strongbox and take the gold. *We risked our hides for that loot,* he felt himself wanting to say. But even in his own mind the words didn't sound true. He never felt at risk during the robbery. And he couldn't remember ever feeling such a strong urge to take the gold after one of Pa's hold-ups. Those moments had always felt wrong to him. He couldn't understand the shift in his feelings now. He felt like Pa's words were trying to come out of him. He felt like Pa's desires were rising up in him. It put a sick feeling in the pit of his stomach.

"Set it down here," Bart said, lowering his side of the box so Cody felt the full weight of its contents before lowering his own end.

Cody shook thoughts of Pa and gold from his mind and knelt down beside the box. He picked up a palm-sized stone with a good edge for digging, and started scraping the dirt with it. Bart did the same. Once they got through the tightly packed top layer, the dirt came away easily, and they soon had a hole large enough to stow the strongbox. They lowered it in and Cody watched Bart push piles of dirt into the opening and over the gold. He thought about the first time he encountered Bart, and how the old man had skulked away with two bags of stolen loot. He couldn't help but wonder about the old man's intentions now.

Bart and Cody walked back towards Fortune City. Cody felt glad they weren't carrying the heavy box any further. He massaged his right arm which was sore from hauling and digging. If Smoke hadn't run off, he'd be riding rather than walking in the heat. Cody still felt surprised – and hurt – that the mustang had deserted him. He knew it was foolish, but he'd thought they were friends. It made him wonder about Bart, too. Sometimes the old man seemed to care for him, but Cody wasn't certain. Leaving the gold made him suspicious. The boy chided himself for caring about such things. He'd always been on his own, and he always would be.

"It don't seem smart to be headin back to town," Cody said. "We didn't even hide our faces during the hold up."

"Just act normal," Bart said. "No one's got any reason to suspect us yet."

"And when they do?"

"Then it will be time."

"Time for what?"

"To get the map."

Bart didn't say anything more, so Cody pulled Sky Weaver's pebble from his pocket. He lay the smooth stone in the middle of his open palm. He let it rest there as he walked. He had given up trying to feel the stone's weight or to raise it into the air. Instead, he just let it sit there in his palm.

He walked and gazed at the Skyscraper, bleak and imposing. King waited somewhere in that building, where he would learn his gold had been stolen and he would rage. Grimshaw and Morgan waited there, too, guns loaded, trigger fingers itching. And Pa. He waited for King to tell him what man to kill or bury next.

Cody tried not to think about these men or what lay ahead. He looked down at the path just ahead of his feet and focused on the scrape of his boots on the dirt. The smell of baked earth. The sun on his neck and the breeze that drew away the heat. His half-extended arm, still and weightless. The bend of his fingers and the creases etched in his half-curled hand. And for a fleeting moment, the stone. He perceived the pebble's smooth surface shifting, vibrating across the skin of his palm. It was the equivalent of looking through a magnifying glass, but not with vision, with touch. Cody felt at once calm and excited. He glanced at Bart, who walked quietly beside him, staring at the distant Skyscraper. He decided not to tell the old man.

Back at the Good Fortune Hotel, Bart and Cody dined in the restaurant. Cody smooshed mashed potatoes under his fork. His fingers gripped the utensil tightly. He squeezed the pebble in his other hand. He listened to bits of conversation at nearby tables. A man planned to set out west in the morning. A woman missed her sister. A young girl told her rag doll a story.

A pretty, middle-aged waitress moved about the room filling glasses from a pitcher of water. She looked at Cody's glass, still full, then looked at Cody and smiled. Her large eyes shone deep brown. Cody smiled back, but her eyes made him sad. As she walked away, he found himself thinking about the man in the coach who Pa had shot dead. He wondered where that man was heading. He wondered if that man left a sister or a wife or a daughter behind. Then Cody thought about his own mother. He thought she must have had eyes like the waitress's. He thought she would smile at nervous boys in restaurants. He felt a tear well in his eye and wiped it away.

Bart sipped tea and watched out the window. Slowly he turned his face towards Cody. Then he picked up his fork and knife, reached across the table and stabbed his fork into the baked chicken that lay untouched on Cody's plate. He cut away a piece of the meat and deposited it into his mouth. He chewed slowly and watched Cody; his face held the hint of a smile, as if he were about to deliver the punch line of a joke.

"Tastes fine," he said finally. "What's the trouble?"

Cody clinked his fork against the surface of his plate. "Just seems like we shouldn't be hanging around town right out in the open."

"If we hide, folks will have more reason to suspect," Bart said. "As long as we don't run into those gents from the coach, we should be fine."

Cody knew it was always best not to act guilty. Pa had taught him that much at least. But even Pa didn't strut back into town after a hold-up. It made Cody wonder if Bart was smarter than Pa, or just crazier. He considered this question for a moment, then shovelled a forkful of mashed potatoes into his mouth. He scowled at Bart, who was watching him eat, still smirking.

"What did that note say?" Cody asked. "The one you gave the coachman?"

Bart laughed. "It said, 'Guess who?'"

Cody frowned. "What's that supposed to mean?"

"It mean's King will know I'm here."

"From the note?"

"That and the description of us those coachmen will give him. They'll be hanging wanted posters all over Fortune City by tomorrow morning. King and I are no strangers."

Cody slept with the pebble tucked in his curled palm. When he woke, he found Bart sitting in a small wooden chair beside the window. He was neatly dressed and sipping a cup of tea. He turned when he heard Cody stir and smiled at the boy.

"Get dressed," he said. "You ought to see this."

Cody rose and pulled on his trousers and boots. He followed Bart down the stairs, through the hotel lobby, and out to the street. He half expected to see Smoke standing by the post outside the hotel, but the horse had not returned. Bart led Cody to a storefront two buildings down. The sun had barely risen, but a steady flow of people were already moving in and out of the shop. A sign above the door said "City Hardware." Cody thought they were going in to buy supplies, but Bart stopped outside the doorway. He nodded towards the wall and Cody followed with his eyes until he saw the poster Bart had promised.

Drawn in black ink was a fair likeness of Bart's face, round chin, small bulbous nose, thin-lipped grin, bowler cap. But the artist couldn't capture the gleam of Bart's green eyes. In the drawing they looked beady and cold. Cody felt offended that the drawing made Bart look like a cold-blooded killer. Above the picture, written on two lines: WANTED, BLACK BART. And below the picture on two lines: REWARD, 5 GOLD BARS.

Cody looked at Bart. Any suspicions he held of the old man melted away. They were up against something bigger than Cody had realized, and they were in it together.

"Did you–" Cody started to say, but Bart held a finger to his lips. He nodded again towards the wall and Cody saw the poster pinned beside Bart's. He felt his stomach drop.

The drawing looked a lot like Pa, piercing eyes, hawkish nose, angular face. And mean. A flat brimmed hat angled down over the brow giving the eyes a sinister stare. The man in the drawing looked like he might kill someone for a nickel. But the face looked younger than Pa's, with smooth unshaven cheeks. And above the picture, written on two lines: WANTED, KID CODY. Below, written on two lines: REWARD, 5 GOLD BARS.

Cody's lungs suddenly felt too tight to breathe. His

thoughts raced too wildly to make sense. He couldn't understand or believe what had happened. He had become Pa. He had followed his father's path. He felt lost. But at the same time he knew this was always the way his life would go. This was always what he would become. Cody was an outlaw.

Chapter 28

THE PLAN

Cody stared at the wanted poster. It felt like a dream, as if the face on the paper wasn't really his, but someone else's face that was supposed to be his. It scared him, but he couldn't look away. He was *wanted*, and some part of him felt like he had accomplished something, however bad it might be. He wondered if feeling that way about it was the same as wishing it happened. Pa, he thought, would probably laugh when he saw the poster. Pa would laugh at the way Cody thought about the world.

"We ought to get out of sight," Bart said. He set a hand on Cody's shoulder.

Cody looked up and nodded. He squeezed the pebble in his palm. He glanced at the poster one last time before following Bart away from the hardware store. Men and women walked along the side of the road, moving in and out of shops. A boy selling newspapers exclaimed the day's headline, "Stage robbed on Blood Hill! Read about it for a nickel!" He held the front page above his head. Cody looked at it and felt the tingle in his fingers. He quickened his pace, but glanced at Bart and found the old man strolling behind, smiling and whistling. He took a breath and slowed himself down. No one seemed to notice them, and they had almost reached the Good Fortune.

But Bart didn't stop at the hotel. He kept walking and led Cody past Thompson's Butcher Shop, the Telegraph Post, and Western Stagecoach Lines. Two red-trimmed coaches, similar to the one Bart and Cody had robbed the day before, sat outside the entrance awaiting the day's passengers. Cody raised a hand to the side of his face so no one inside the office would recognize him.

"Ain't we going back to the hotel?" he said.

Bart smiled and shook his head. "I checked us out while you were sleeping," he said. "Before someone took notice."

Cody felt reassured that Bart was at least paying attention. They passed a few more shops and finally reached a cross street where a small green sign in the shape of an arrow pointed down the narrow road. Neat white letters on the arrow read, "McManus Boarding Stables." Bart turned down the road and Cody followed. A short distance ahead they found a broad wooden building with large open windows every 10 or so feet. A single set of double doors, which were latched wide open, provided the only entrance to the structure.

Inside, a row of horse stalls lined each side of the central aisle, and most of them were full. They walked past a tall skinny man with a thick brown moustache mucking an empty stall. He looked up at them and nodded as they passed. Bart tipped his bowler and kept moving. He stopped at one of the last stalls on the right. The dark bay mare stood inside with its nose sticking out the square window opening. Cody felt a hint of disappointment when he didn't find Smoke standing beside the mare. Bart unlatched the gate and they stepped in with the horse.

A sack of oats slumped in the corner. Bart untied it and reached into it. He fed the mare from his hand, patting the horse's neck with his other hand. Cody sat down on a low, three-legged stool against the wall. He listened to the sound of horses snorting and whinnying. He breathed the smell of horse and wet hay.

"Pa must know I'm here," he said finally.

"Seems likely." Bart tilted his head thoughtfully, but didn't say more.

"He'll look for me," Cody said. "He always looks for me. He always finds me."

Cody took off his hat and dragged his fingers roughly through his tangled hair. He couldn't understand how he had come so far and still ended up in the same city with Pa. Tangled in the same mess with Pa. An outlaw like Pa. He even looked like Pa.

"What are we going to do?" he said.

Bart stroked the mare's dark neck. He smiled mildly as if it were any other day. "King also knows we're here," he said. He looked at Cody and raised his eyebrows as if the conclusion were obvious.

"And?" Cody said irritably. He felt the muscles in his shoulders tighten. He clenched the pebble in his hand.

"Now we draw him out."

Cody felt a stab of anger in his gut. He couldn't understand how Bart seemed so casual, like nothing was happening. He closed his eyes and leant his head forwards. He tugged at his hair with his fingers. He took a deep breath and spoke through clenched teeth. "Why do we do that?" he said. "Why is that a good thing? Do you want Pa to find me?"

Bart didn't smile now. He just looked at Cody thoughtfully.

"It might be good to face your pa again."

"Last time I faced Pa, he bashed in my face."

Bart nodded, his green eyes set seriously on Cody's. "Let's just see what happens."

Cody broke Bart's gaze and looked down at the hay scattered across the floor. For the first time, he realized that Bart didn't always have the answers. It wasn't that he had thought Bart knew everything, but until now he couldn't recall him not knowing how to handle a situation.

The old man had always seemed to know what was going to happen before it did. He always seemed to know what to say or do. Now, with Pa involved, Bart seemed less sure. In a way, it made Cody feel better, like he wasn't an idiot for getting tripped up by Pa, for not always knowing the right thing to do – but it also worried him. He took a deep breath.

"Stand up," Bart said, stretching a hand down to help Cody up. He looked out the window and Cody did the same. The Skyscraper dominated their view, its cold grey structure a block of ice against the cool blue sky.

"Where do you suppose the map is?" Bart said.

Cody's eyes scanned the building. He watched the

crows rise from and settle on its bony ledges. Some flew down below his view, where he knew the bank stood like a fortress, armed guard on its rooftop.

"In the bank?" he said.

"Possibly, but more likely in the Skyscraper," Bart said. "King won't want to lose the map again. He'll keep it close at hand. Somewhere at the top. Wherever he spends his time."

"It's a big place," Cody said. "Maybe we can sneak in. Maybe we can even find the map. But how do we get near it?"

"We draw King and his gang out."

Cody looked up at the Skyscraper's sinister window eyes. It was a long way up and they'd have to pass a lot of people along the way, gang or no gang. "Can't you make us unseen?" he said.

Bart shook his head. "Not while we're moving."

Cody turned and looked at Bart. He reached out and stroked the mare's back. "So how do we get them out of the Skyscraper?"

Bart smiled and his green eyes glinted. "Easy," he said. "We rob the bank."

Chapter 29

SHOTGUN SHELLS

Bart held a shotgun shell close to his nose and peered at it squint-eyed as he slipped the curved tip of his pocket knife into the papered top of the small cardboard cylinder.

"The gunman on the roof won't matter," Cody said. "You'll be dead before you get out of the bank. Every man in there will have a six-gun."

Bart glanced at the boy and grinned. "That's why I intend to work real quiet."

Cody shook his head and scowled at the old man. He had a bad feeling like he did before one of Pa's hold-ups. The difference was that Cody felt worried about what might happen to Bart. With Pa he worried what might happen to someone else.

The stable was quiet now. Earlier, a few men had come to pick up their horses and another man had dropped one off. But no one had paid any mind to Bart and Cody standing in the stall with the dark bay mare.

At one point, McManus, the stable man, stopped by and asked if he should muck out the stall. Bart said no need as they would be leaving soon. He held out a handful of gold coins.

"I appreciate the extra storage," he said.

McManus glanced down at the coins and his thick moustache rose with a smile. "No trouble at all," he said. Then he walked away, whistling and drumming the handle of his shovel.

Bart stepped to the end of the stall where the sack of oats slumped in the corner. With two hands, he grabbed the lip of the burlap sack and dragged it across the hard-packed dirt floor. Where the sack had been, the dirt rose in a slight mound with deep heel marks stomped into it. Bart knelt and dug at the dirt with his fingers, exposing a square, earth-stained board. He picked up the board to reveal a narrow cavity dug into the ground.

From the hole, Bart lifted a shotgun and handed it to Cody. "Set this against the wall," he said. Then he lay on the ground and reached his arm deeper into the hole. He drew out a box of shotgun shells and set them by the stool. He reached in again and drew out a small sack tied shut with twine. He plopped it down beside the shells and it made a sizzling, shifting sound.

Now, Bart sat on the three-legged stool staring at the shotgun shell. Cody stood beside the mare and stroked the horse's dark nose as he watched the old man work. He gripped the pebble tightly in his free hand.

Bart sliced and pried open the top of the shell. He dumped out the steel shots, which clattered off the leg of the stool and landed in the dirt and hay. He shook the cylinder and a few more shots dropped into the dirt. Then he shook it by his ear to make sure it was empty.

Bart nodded and set the empty shell on the floor beside the wall. He pulled a second shell from the box, lifted it close to his nose, and peered at it.

"I don't think you should go in alone," Cody said, his hand now motionless on the mare's nose.

"I'll fit right in. Just another merchant making a withdrawal." Bart raised his knife to the shell. "Only the banker will see my gun."

Cody appraised the old man in his neat black suit, black shoes, black bowler and white shirt. "You do look like a banker," he said. "But folks will recognize you. Don't forget the posters."

Bart drew his blade away from the shell and looked

up at Cody. "I remember the posters. And they will too. I'm counting on it." He smiled broadly and his green eyes glinted. "But before that happens, they'll look at me funny. They'll wonder why I look familiar." Bart closed his mouth as if content to stop there.

"And?" Cody said impatiently. The mare snorted, and he lifted his hand from the horse's warm coat.

"When the banker yells 'thief!' and alarm bells ring," Bart said, "they'll all put it together, the whole bank full of em. That's what will draw King out of his fortress."

"How much gold you think you can carry?"

"Only need one small bag," Bart said. "It's not the gold. It's the idea of stealing it right under his nose. King will have to react swiftly. He'll want to make an example. More so when he knows it's me."

Cody's eyes narrowed and he lifted off his wide brimmed hat. "And why is that?"

"We've got history."

"I suppose I knew that," Cody said. He watched Bart use the tip of his knife blade to carefully pry open the top of the second shell. The old man tipped the cylinder and the small steel shots dripped down like grey rain drops, landing in quick succession and bouncing away in low arcs.

"You'll probably only get to fire off two of these,"

Bart said, "but I'll make a second pair just in case."

Cody nodded. According to the plan, after Bart robbed the bank, King's men would chase him and he would draw them East while Cody slipped into the Skyscraper to find the map. It seemed to Cody that there was a lot of space to hide a map inside the Skyscraper, but Bart was convinced he could find it in one of the upper rooms. "You'll know the one when you get there," he said.

Bart set down the second empty shell and began working on a third. "I've stolen a lot of King's gold," he said. "I don't like the man's greed. I don't like the way he squeezes money from folks who don't have enough to begin with. Steal from the rich. I can accept that. But don't steal from the poor."

Cody's mind instantly went to the Ryders. He thought of the fine lamps and furniture in their home. He didn't think they were rich. But they were far from poor. Did Bart think it was right to steal from them? They worked hard for what they had.

Steel shots clinked off the leg of the stool and fell to the ground. Bart put the third shell beside the others and lifted one more.

"King and I knew each other a long time ago," he said. "Before he was King and I was Black Bart."

"You were friends?" Cody felt a pulse of distrust rise in him.

Bart shook his head. "Not exactly friends. We did things together."

"And then?"

"At some point we stopped agreeing on how to do things." Bart emptied the fourth shell and the steel shots scattered across the floor. He held up the empty cylinder to Cody. "This shell," he said, "always has the potential to be dangerous. But it depends on what you fill it with."

Bart reached down and lifted the small sack that he had taken from the storage hole. He untied the twine from around the throat of the sack and slipped his fingers into the opening. He drew out his hand and Cody saw small, golden, shrivelled kernels of corn – chicken feed.

The kernels lay in the palm of Bart's hand that also held the shell. With his free hand, he pinched a kernel between his fingers and inserted it through the small opening in the top of the shell. He did this once and again, pressing one kernel at a time through the small space. He worked slowly and carefully, but picked up speed as he went. Finally, he pushed in a final kernel and closed the paper flaps. With his thumb over the top, he shook the shell. It didn't rattle as it did with the steel shot, but Cody could hear the corn shifting inside the shell.

Now Bart looked at Cody and his eyes glinted. He raised the shell then motioned with it towards the floor, which was pocked with tiny grey balls. "Those steel shots will kill a man," he said. "This won't kill anyone."

"The rifleman on the roof?" Cody said. "That's how I'm going to keep him from murdering you? With corn shot?"

Bart smiled and nodded. "Won't kill him, but it will sting like a hornet."

Cody rolled his eyes and sighed. "Did somebody fill your shell of a head with crazy?"

Bart laughed. "Could be," he said. "But it will work."

Bart lifted a second shell and started to fill it with corn kernels.

Cody watched him for a time, then turned and stared out at the Skyscraper. He wondered what he'd find inside.

Chapter 30

THE BANK ROBBERY

Obscured from view by the half-wall that surrounded the rooftop, the man seemed to glide above the bank, the barrel of his rifle hovering before him like a cold, dangerous bird. He stared at the cloudy leaden sky and occasionally glanced down at the road. His tall brown hat hung behind him by a loose cord around his neck and when the wind gusted the hat flew up and then banged down on his back. He huddled inside his shirt and leant into the wind. From the brooding Skyscraper above, crows swooped down on arcs of strong wind. Distant black clouds raced towards him.

Cody leant against the wall of the telegraph office across the street. He watched the rifleman, and tried to look natural despite the double barrel shotgun hidden under the long leather coat he wore. Beneath the heavy garment, the weapon hung by a frayed rope that dug into his shoulder. The butt of the rifle pressed against his chest. The barrel jabbed at his ankles.

Cody felt keenly aware of the steel weapon's weight against his chest. His breath came short and his fingers tingled. He forced himself not to reach inside the coat to reposition the gun every time he breathed. His eyes flitted over suited men who walked with purpose in and out of the telegraph office but didn't bother to glance at him. He pressed his grey hat tightly down on his head.

Cody could see the bank's entrance at a sharp angle from where he stood. A thin man tugged on the handle of the thick brass door, leaning back to get his weight into the effort. The door opened slowly and Cody edged forwards, looking and listening for some sign of Bart. It seemed to Cody that the old man had been inside much too long.

The dark bay mare stood by a post outside the bank beside several other saddled horses. Its rope was draped over the rail but not tied. It stomped its front hooves in a slow, steady rhythm and sniffed the air and snorted.

On the rooftop, the rifleman's face looked dark and vague, but his eyes were large and white as moons with distinct dark centres, and Cody could clearly read their movement. The man put the rifle to his shoulder and aimed overhead at the swooping crows. His eyes and the rifle's barrel moved in unison from crow to crow. He shifted his aim in tight, quick motions. He didn't pull the trigger, but Cody suspected he could gun down every black bird in the sky without wasting a bullet.

Then a bell pealed and the man's eyes darted to the road. In a single smooth movement, his body pivoted and glided forwards, his rifle swung out over the wall. His head titled sideways and down towards the barrel and one eye closed. He became very still.

Cody's heart pounded in time with the clanging bell. His mind went cloudy. His hands felt thick and numb as he reached inside his coat.

The bank's massive brass door twitched.

Cody felt the shotgun barrel cold and heavy in his hand. As he pulled the weapon from his coat, the door swung wide as if Cody's motion had pulled it open.

Thunder echoed from inside the bank and the bell clanged frantically.

Crows cawed.

Cody's heart pounded and he felt the buzz of blood racing through his body. The wind poured against his face but barely reached his lungs.

Through the bank's open doorway, the tip, then

the sole, then the top of Bart's boot became visible. His black-clad leg slipped through the opening, followed by his bowler hat clutched in his fist, the length of an arm, chest, round face. Then his trailing leg, black trousers spattered dark with blood. He dragged the leg through the door, a pained, hitched limp. He hobbled towards the dark bay mare, a stuffed white sack gripped tightly in his fingers.

On the rooftop, the rifleman held motionless as Bart moved into his view. Crows swirled and cawed above him. Wind gusted.

Cody set the shotgun to his shoulder and raised the barrel. He aimed the weapon at the man on the rooftop. Felt the hard curved triggers against his finger.

Lightning flashed brightly and in the brief blindness that followed, Cody saw an image of the Okwaho warrior falling from the rooftop. Blood spewed from his chest. Cody shut his eyes and shook the memory from his mind.

Rain began to fall.

Cody took a breath and pulled the first trigger. The gun blasted as if it meant to kill someone and the butt slammed into his shoulder. Corn shot flew from the weapon towards the roof, rose like a swarm of bees, arced towards the rifleman, then curled away. The small golden shrapnel caught in a sharp gust of wind and stalled in the air, short of the wall, and fell two stories to the ground. Cody swore under his breath. Every inch of his body buzzed now. The knot uncoiled in his stomach. The plan was a disaster and Bart was going to die.

A crowd of armed men clambered from the bank.

Bart reached the mare and stepped with his good leg into the stirrup.

The rifleman's white eye trained itself on the old bank robber. The barrel of his rifle followed obediently.

Bart's body rose above the saddle.

The rifleman inhaled deeply.

In the instant before he exhaled and squeezed the trigger, Cody jerked his own trigger. The gunpowder erupted and corn shot blasted out of the barrel towards the rifleman. It cut through the swirls of wind and sailed above the rooftop. The kernels pelted the crows over the man's head and fell down on him like harmless, golden rain. The man didn't flinch, but stopped long enough to glance down at the corn scattered on the rooftop.

Bart swung his bloody leg over the mare and dropped into the saddle. He grabbed and tugged the reins to steer the horse away from the bank.

The rifleman's white eye again settled on Bart. Again, he set himself and inhaled deeply. Cody knew he was about to pull the trigger – and he knew the bullet would find its mark and Bart would be dead. But before that could happen, a swarm of crows swooped down on the rifleman in a great commotion. A blur of black wings slashed and swirled around him as the greedy birds fought for the corn shot scattered at his feet.

The dark bay mare turned.

Cody cracked open the shotgun.

Cawing birds mobbed the rifleman.

Rain sliced down through the sky.

The mare leapt forwards.

The crowd of men from the bank surged towards the street.

Thunder cracked.

Cody shook the empty shells from his gun, but too late.

A shot echoed. A flash from the rooftop.

Bart's body jerked and dark crimson sprayed from his back. He flopped forwards in his saddle and his chest dropped against the mare's neck.

Cody lost his breath. His mind tried to think a hundred thoughts at once and went blank. He wrestled the rope from his shoulder and threw the shotgun to the ground.

The dark bay mare galloped down the road.

Cody darted behind the telegraph office and ran behind the shops in the direction Bart had ridden.

Chapter 31

SHOWDOWN

Rain sliced down like long scars on the grey sky. Bart sat hunched in his saddle, the dark bay mare stopped in the middle of the street, its hooves scraping at the wet, packed dirt nervously. Ten men, still and silent atop muscular horses, blocked the road west. Gus Grimshaw and a half dozen riders blocked the road east. They waited in their saddles, grim-faced, rain dripping from the brims of their hats, guns drawn.

Bart took a breath and drew himself up in his saddle. He tugged the reins and spun his mare towards the alley where Cody now stood. The horse coiled on its back legs to spring forward. Then Bart's eyes fell on the boy and their spark went dim. He tugged hard at the reins and the horse danced another half-turn on its back legs before leaping towards the opposite side of the street. The bay took two steps before a shot blasted from a nearby rooftop. The blast echoed down in jagged pieces like shattered glass. A puff of dark fur and blood spurted from the mare's chest, and the horse plunged nose-first into the dirt and tumbled forwards. Bart lurched from the saddle and sailed into the rain-cut sky.

Cody felt himself tense as Bart flew skywards, but the old man's body seemed to relax. His arms spread wide like a bird's and he hung like a feather on the breeze. His legs, which initially trailed behind him, swung slowly forwards until they aligned beneath his body, and he stepped lightly to the ground as if descending a staircase. He continued forwards and ducked behind a trio of potbellied stoves, which stood beneath an awning outside the hardware store.

With the exception of Grimshaw, the men from both ends of the street edged their horses towards the store and formed a loose semicircle around Bart's position. Pa was not among them. Morgan, too, was absent but Cody knew his shot had cut down the mare.

Grimshaw's dark, cold eyes scanned the scene. His men raised their guns and started firing. Their bullets shattered the hardware store windows and filled the wooden walls of the squat building with pockets of lead.

The wrought-iron stoves that protected Bart, sparked and pinged as bullets ricocheted off them. The men fired until their chambers were empty, and Cody held his breath until the last hammer clicked down harmlessly.

The men then looked to Grimshaw, who stared back and spat, his jaw set in a sneer. The shadow of his hat angled sharply across his face hiding one eye in darkness. He raised a palm to his men, who nodded and dropped their gazes to their empty six-shooters. They opened the steel chambers and spilled the spent cartridges onto the road. They leant forwards in their saddles, trying to keep the rain off their ammunition as they reloaded.

Grimshaw peered down the street, his eyes hawkish. He looked to the rooftop of the Good Fortune Hotel and nodded. Cody couldn't see Morgan, but he knew the rifleman was there. He knew he couldn't reach Bart without Morgan seeing.

The rain weighed down Cody's long coat, and he shrugged it off and let it drop in a heavy heap at his feet. The wind bit through his shirt, but he welcomed the freedom of movement. He knew he should be at the Skyscraper already, searching for the map, but he couldn't leave Bart. He watched the row of stoves across the street looking for movement. He feared the stillness was a sign of Bart's death. He wondered what Grimshaw was waiting for.

Then a small figure appeared at the west end of the street, a rider in black, a shadow against the leaden sky. He moved forwards slowly, his small black horse gliding over the road like a dark spirit. Cody knew the man was King before he could see him clearly.

Grimshaw nudged his horse forwards and stopped behind the row of gunmen. He waited, hands resting on the horn of his saddle, as King rode towards him. The other men turned in their saddles to watch. Cody edged towards the corner of the building. He watched all the men staring at King, the black rider and black horse slowly growing larger and closer like a shadow in dying daylight.

Cody reached down and gripped the handle of his Colt, drew it from the holster and pressed it against his chest. He took a deep breath, crouched low and skittered into the road. He felt himself trying to hide behind the rain. In his mind, he asked Big Sky to bend the light around his body. He could feel the rain and the wind and the cold, and he tried to feel the light among them. He could not, but he felt the time, which slowed in his mind to a crawl. He felt the distance, which grew to an impossibly great expanse. He felt the beat of his heart and the sweat on his brow, the hair that stood on the back of his neck, the tightness of his jaw, the space between each step and the scuff of his boots on the packed dirt, which seemed to vibrate faintly beneath his feet.

King pulled up beside Grimshaw. The two outlaws conferred and Grimshaw pointed towards the row of stoves. Cody was halfway across the street. He froze and waited a breath. He watched King turn his cold eyes towards Bart. No one seemed to notice Cody. If he was going to get to Bart, he had to move now. He ducked his head and closed his eyes. He sprang forwards with all his strength. His legs pushed off from the dirt, and his body jerked into a sudden run.

One step, and then another. All he heard was the rain, the pounding of his boots. Felt the lift of the wind. Felt the sky. Felt his spirit swell. He was going to reach his friend. Somehow in the pressure of the moment, it came clearly to his mind that Bart was his friend, despite whatever doubts or fears he felt, Bart was his friend. Now he had to reach the old man. Not to tell him how he felt. Maybe not even to save him. He feared it might already be too late. But he had to reach Bart now that he understood. To look him in the eye. As friends.

Then a distant shot rang from above and clipped the dirt just ahead of Cody's boots. He fell and tumbled sideways, instinctively. He rolled to his knees and opened his eyes. He was only a few steps from the edge of the road.

Grimshaw turned on his mount and glared at Cody. His stubbled cheek rose and his lip curled in a vicious snarl. "Don't you take another step," he commanded.

Cody sank lower to the ground. He didn't drop his gun, but set it against his thigh.

Grimshaw spat and raised his chin. He shouted into the rainy sky. "If he moves, drain his heart."

Cody knew Morgan was listening, and somewhere in the dim sky, his rifle was pointed at Cody's chest. He felt the knot uncoil in his stomach. The chill of the wind.

Grimshaw looked at Cody again as if he meant to say something more, but King spoke and the outlaw turned back towards the hardware store where Bart lay hidden or dead behind the wrought-iron stoves. King rode forwards and his gunmen nudged their horses aside.

"Bart, my old companion," King said loudly, "it doesn't have to end this way."

He waited for a reply. Stared ahead calmly. Pulled his black gloves snug on his hands.

"You could join me. There are fortunes to be made."

There was a long silence. Then Bart's voice rang out. "You can't believe that, Tyrus."

King's grip tightened on his reins. "I believe you can still choose to see reason."

"And help you plunder the Freelands?"

"It beats petty thievery, Bart."

"Does it? Because you call it business?"

"I'll have to kill you. And this boy." King looked at Cody, his face grim and tight-lipped.

"You know I'm prepared to die," Bart shouted. "So is the boy."

King's mouth curled slowly to a grin.

Cody felt a violent buzz rush through his body. He wasn't prepared to die. The ground beneath his feet began to shake.

Chapter 32

WAR CRIES

The ground quaked and a rumble climbed into Cody's boots and through his body and shook his bones and teeth and skull. Small rocks vibrated over the road, leaping and bouncing off the wet dirt like small insects. A clamour of pounding hooves thundered in the sky like war drums, drowning out the howling wind and rattling downpour. Deep grunts and growls surged against the storm. Crows cawed. Lightning flashed. Thunder echoed. The sky darkened.

Then a heartbeat of silence.

A crimson flash.

Dark outline of a Tatanka. Tall, shadowed rider. Spear in hand, cocked behind his shoulder. A sudden jerk of his arm. A sharp, edge-thin sound and the spear streaking forwards, slicing the wind, piercing raindrops. The stone point punctured a man's chest, shattering one rib and pushing past another before plunging into his heart, which burst like a thousand raindrops. The man's eyes widened for an instant before he slumped forward and dropped from his saddle to the mud.

Bear Claw Man watched his enemy fall. He let out a piercing war cry, the muscles and veins of his neck taut against his earthy skin. He reached back and grabbed a spear from the quiver strapped to his buffalo's flank.

Sky Weaver charged in behind the tall warrior, his buffalo lurching and crashing forwards in a thunderous, stomping gallop. Clenched in one fist above his head, he held a buffalo horn streaked with indigo paint. He slashed it through the sky and a streak of lightning, long and glowing, sliced down from a dark storm cloud and struck Tyrus King with a great sizzling hiss. The expelled breath from King's lungs thudded like a hammer blow. His body jerked backwards out of his saddle as if a massive hawk had flung him to the sky. He sailed and landed hard in the road, tumbling to a stop, limbs bent awkwardly, unmoving. A thin ribbon of smoke rose from his flesh.

Grimshaw sneered and fired a series of shots that sent the two Tatanka warriors turning defensively.

He shouted orders to his gunmen, who stared, dazed, at King's limp body, but came awake at the sound of Grimshaw's voice. They started firing at the Tatanka and at Cody, who had not moved from where he crouched in the road. Gunshots flared orange in the grey sky and bullets ricocheted off the dirt. Cody scampered on hands and knees through the mud and dove into an alley alongside the butcher shop.

He spat dirt from his lips and wiped mud from his eyes. He lay his back against the wall and tried to catch his breath, which came fast and shallow in sync with his racing heartbeat. He could smell gun smoke and the tinge of blood and burnt flesh. He looked down at the Colt in his hand, heavy and cold and wet. He cracked open the cylinder, spun it to see it was loaded, and snapped it shut. He inhaled deeply and peeked around the corner.

Bart lay in the dirt, two stores down, bloody and writhing, gun in hand. Just beyond the stoves that protected him, half a dozen gunmen still hovered, their arms outstretched, blasting shots at the Tatanka warriors. The other gunmen had scattered across the road on nervous horses. Two men lay on the ground with spears sticking from bloody bellies.

Grimshaw crouched on the ground now beside King.

He scooped the man's limp body and flung it over the back of his horse. He leapt into the saddle, galloped eastwards down the road and disappeared around a corner.

Cody crawled from his hiding place and dashed towards Bart. He ducked his head with each shot that echoed. His boots pounded the mud and he felt the wind pushing against him. As he neared the hardware store he dove forwards and crawled on his belly until he reached the old man.

Bart looked up. His green eyes glinted dimly. "Do you have the map?" he said.

Cody felt the breath catch in his throat. He looked at Bart and smiled thinly. He nodded. "Yeah. I got it." He moved close to the old man and cradled his head in his hands. Bart's skin looked pale and thin and brittle. A dark patch of blood spread across his black jacket. Another patch seeped from his thigh. The blood there dripped from his knee and formed a small, dark puddle in the dirt.

Bart's voice was faint and distant. "The Tatanka came?"

Cody nodded. He looked to the street. King's men were edging away to the west. Their eyes looked crazed and confused like injured horses. They fired again and again, but moved steadily backwards. Bear Claw Man swung his spear and pushed them back, his eyes wild and fearless. Sky Weaver moved slow and deliberate; he seemed to push the wind and rain harder in the gunmen's direction.

"Give them the map," Bart said. "Go with them."

In the street, Cody heard the clash continue. Gunshots and war cries. The sizzle of spears through the sky and the thud of flesh falling to the ground. He looked at Bart's eyes, now dim and cloudy as wisps of smoke from a dying fire. He reached into his pocket and drew out the pebble Sky Weaver had given him. He gripped it tightly and tried to feel its magic, some life he could pass to Bart, some flame he could stoke, some weight he could lift. But all he felt was the stone and the weight of his heart.

Bart smiled at him like nothing was wrong.

"Are you going to die?" Cody asked. "Don't die."

Bart's green eyes glinted.

Rain poured down.

Guns fired.

Then a rumble rose from the ground and shook Cody. A dank smell reached his nostrils. Dirt sprayed his face as a great, wet, stinking buffalo lumbered to a stop at his feet. Atop the beast sat the old Tatanka, Map

Dreamer. He studied Bart and then looked at Cody. He climbed down from his muscled mount. His eyes held no despair.

"Help me lift him," he said. "I will take him."

Cody felt hope rise in his chest like a deep breath of fresh air or a swell of laughter.

He grabbed Bart by one arm, and Map Dreamer grabbed the other. They heaved his body onto the buffalo's back and pushed him forwards to balance him there. Cody kept hold of the old man's arm to steady him.

"Where will you take him?" he asked.

"We know men who can heal him," Map Dreamer said.

"Still?"

Map Dreamer nodded and Cody's hopefulness grew.

Then a shot echoed from high above.

A heartbeat of silence.

Cody looked at his body unsure if he had been hit. He looked at Bart, already bloody and dying. Then Map Dreamer. The old warrior stared at Cody. A gurgle of blood seeped from his neck. He held Cody's gaze with sad, defeated eyes and slumped to the ground.

Chapter 33

NEAR DEATH

Cody heard the wolves just as Bart slid off the buffalo's back and fell to the ground. His chest and one side of his face sank into the mud. His eyes lay closed. No part of him moved. Cody dropped to his knees and rolled the old man to his back.

"Be alive," he whispered, grabbing him by the shoulders and shaking him. "Wake up."

Bart didn't stir.

Cody holstered his Colt. He climbed to his feet, crouched low and slipped his arms under Bart's. He tried to lift him, but the old man felt so heavy that Cody thought he might already be dead. He heaved, straining the muscles in his legs and back, and managed to pin Bart's limp body against the buffalo's flank. But the beast moaned and turned, and Bart's weight shifted and slid through Cody's arms, slumping back to the ground. The buffalo, meanwhile, stuck its snout into Sky Weaver's belly and nudged him.

"He's already dead," Cody said, his voice cracking with stress. "Let me help Bart."

The buffalo continued to prod the old Tatanka warrior.

Cody shook Bart again. He felt a shiver build in his fingers and creep up his forearms. He felt his heart begin to race and his breath grow shallow. In the pit of his stomach, he felt Bart's life fading.

Then he felt hot breath on his neck. The smell of raw meat and blood. A long, low growl.

Cody drew one hand away from Bart's shoulder and touched his fingers to the handle of his Colt. "I'm sorry we failed," he said. "Thanks for teaching me to fish."

He touched the old man's cheek, then spun and blasted a shot at the wolf. The beast jerked backwards with a yelp and tumbled away.

Behind the wolf stood an Okwaho warrior, face and chest smeared with blood, tomahawk clutched in his fist. The knot uncoiled savagely in Cody's stomach. He pulled the trigger of his Colt and the gun boomed and flashed. The warrior dove away and Cody ran.

In the street, Okwaho and wolves surrounded Bear Claw Man and Sky Weaver. A spear flew. A flash lit the grey sky. Wolves and warriors lurched and leapt towards their foes. Howls and cries. Grunts and snarls. Screeches.

Cody ran away from the melee. He risked a glance back to locate the Okwaho who chased him. He flung his arm back and fired a shot. He ran harder. His boots slid and slipped in the mud. He charged around a corner and stumbled forwards, slammed into a wall, but kept running. He could hear the footsteps of the Okwaho warrior slapping lightly after him, growing closer.

Then he *felt* a tomahawk spinning through the air behind him. He dove to the ground and heard the weapon fly over his head. He watched the stone blade cleave itself deeply in a wooden door.

Cody rolled to his back to face the charging warrior. He clutched the handle of his Colt and aimed, but the Okwaho was in the air by then, nearly upon him. And then he was above Cody. He seemed to hover there – grabbed the gun, twisted it from Cody's grip and flung it away. Then he rolled and flipped to his feet as if he had not touched the ground at all.

Cody turned to rise, but the Okwaho leapt to him and gripped him around the neck. His strong fingers squeezed and Cody felt his airway close. He fell back and slammed against the wet ground. Above him the warrior's eyes stared wildly, his lips curled back, baring jagged teeth, and a sound like a wolf's growl rose from his throat. Cody swung his fists. The breath drained from his lungs and he gasped to refill them. He pounded the warrior's arms and jerked his body, trying to throw the man off. But the warrior held tightly and slammed his knee into Cody's belly. The remaining air in Cody's lungs burst out and he felt a sharp pain in his chest. His head felt light and he saw small bright flashes between his face and the warrior's. He tried to punch, but his arms felt limp like ropes. The Okwaho's fingers tightened and the veins on his forearms bulged.

The flashes in Cody's eyes grew larger and more frequent, while the space around them grew darker. He could barely see the warrior now, the hazy features of his face, the faint outline of his arms. He could barely feel the fingers around his throat, which seemed like a distant event, or his own arms, which seemed to belong to someone else. He could barely hear the hoof beats. He could not see the grey mustang rise up behind the Okwaho and slam its hooves down on the warrior's back.

Cool air rushed painfully and wonderfully into

Cody's lungs and his heart beat wildly. He opened his eyes and saw the Okwaho warrior squirming on the ground, pinned there by the horse's hoof.

"Smoke," he said. "It's about time."

The mustang nickered and bobbed its head.

Cody sat up and rubbed his eyes as control came back to his mind and body.

The Okwaho reached for him, but Smoke leant on the man and his arms shot back towards his body.

Cody climbed to his feet. He walked to his pistol, lifted it from the mud, and wiped it clean with his shirtsleeve. He stared down at the Okwaho, grunting and struggling wildly against the horse's weight. He thought about how close he had come to dying and an anger rose inside him. Without his even realizing, he pointed the gun at the warrior's head. His finger glided along the curved edge of the trigger, applying the slightest amount of force, and the weapon yielded to the pressure, moving closer towards its purpose. Cody's feelings raged. He hated the savage before him, hated what he had almost done. The Okwaho didn't deserve to live. Not this one.

Not any of them. Cody knew this in his mind. Felt it in his heart.

But the gun felt heavy and cold in his hand.

The trigger felt dangerous, as if he, too, might die if he pulled it. Pa, he knew, would have already killed the man.

Cody closed his eyes and breathed deeply. He thought of Mrs Ryder and the baby that would soon be born, the world where she would live. He remembered his mother, somewhere beyond this world. He wondered what things he would tell her when they finally met. He didn't want this to be one of them.

Cody lowered his gun and stepped towards Smoke. He set his boot close to the Okwaho's ribs. The warrior glared at him but didn't flinch. Cody reached up and curled his hand over the top of Smoke's neck. Then he half-leapt, half-hoisted himself onto the horse's back. It felt right to be on top of the mustang again.

He grabbed Smoke's reins loosely. "Git up," he said with a touch of his heels to the horse's flanks.

Smoke set off and quickly reached Main Street, where the Okwaho and Tatanka still battled. Cody leaned and tugged the reins to steer the horse eastwards, where Bart still lay in the mud outside the hardware store. Maybe alive. But Smoke turned to the west. He set at a hard gallop down the middle of the street. Cody shifted his weight lower to keep his balance and inhaled deeply. He was along for the ride now.

Ahead, the Skyscraper loomed tall and dangerous, its greedy maw ready to swallow them into darkness. Somewhere a crow cawed.

Chapter 34

THE SKYSCRAPER

The Skyscraper's mouth stretched wide enough and tall enough for half a dozen covered wagons to roll through at once. The opening, which looked completely dark at a distance, glowed dimly within from oil lamps in wall sconces. To one side stood rows of horse stalls tended by booted men with rakes and shovels. In the far corner, men repaired broken wagon frames and reattached missing wheels. In the central area, twenty or so wagons were loaded and unloaded by men in cowhide gloves. They carried bundles, packages and crates from the wagons and loaded them onto two wooden platforms set on the floor and roped through broad openings in the ceiling. Donkeys on the ground pulled the lines to raise the freight to the next level.

Cody couldn't believe the amount of activity and the number of men inside.

Tall doorways in the middle of each wall led to darkened staircases. Through one of these passages, slim men carried stacks of paper to and from the wagons. In front of a second doorway, a tall, square-shouldered man stood. He wore a holster with a pair of shining pistols and leant against the wall, watching two workers lead a team of horses away from a wagon towards the stables. Cody knew the passage behind the gunman was the one he needed to follow.

He slid down from Smoke's back and patted the horse's neck. They stood together just inside the Skyscraper's dark maw. No one seemed to pay them any attention.

"You wait here," Cody said. He patted the horse's neck again, still unsure how he planned to get past the guard.

Smoke snorted quietly.

"I've got to head up, and you'd bring too much attention."

Another soft snort.

"I know, but I don't think you can help this time."

Cody turned and walked towards the guard. He moved casually as if he belonged there, though the pace of his heart quickened with each step. He would tell the man that Grimshaw had sent him to retrieve a package. He tried to think of what questions the man might ask so he could be ready with responses, but neither the questions nor the answers came to him.

Now the guard looked up and regarded Cody, who gave a slight nod to acknowledge the man. He forced himself to maintain his pace and hold the man's gaze. Two more steps. Suddenly the man's eyes widened. Cody heard racing hoof beats close behind and turned just as Smoke bolted past. The mustang charged directly at the guard, a plume of dust rising from its hooves, head craned downward, set to ram. The man blurted an oath, turned, and ran. Smoke whinnied loudly and chased him until he dove behind a stack of crates. Then the mustang circled out into the loading area and weaved in and out of the wagons. The man popped up behind the crates with his gun drawn. He levelled his arm to shoot, but aimed back and forth unsteadily as the horse zigzagged through the busy area. The workers stopped and watched the whinnying mustang run.

Cody stepped quickly through the unguarded doorway. He watched Smoke bolt towards the building's exit, then turned and ran up the staircase, which rose without an exit for what seemed like forever. When he finally reached the top floor his legs felt as limp and heavy as sacks of mud. He stepped onto the landing and stood before a dark walnut door with a heavy brass knob. He took a deep breath to catch some air and drew the Colt from its holster. He stepped forwards and turned the knob, surprised when it turned and clicked. He pushed the door open a crack and peaked through the space.

The room, dimly lit with table lamps turned low, covered the entire length and width of the Skyscraper. A massive chandelier made of hundreds of dangling crystal raindrops hung at the centre of the high ceiling. A maze of leather furniture, tall bookcases and racks of guns and knives spread across the polished oak floor. A long, walnut bar stood off to one side.

Cody didn't see anyone inside. He put his ear by the opening, but only heard the sound of the wind and rain against the windows and the dark melodies of the crows. He pushed the door slowly open and, still seeing no one inside, stepped into the room. He scanned the broad space as he closed the door behind him. Long, split windows stretched nearly the full length of the east and west walls. He couldn't help but step forwards to the window and gaze out. The storm clouds seemed closer and the wind howled louder here. The black birds swarmed outside, riding the churning wind. Cody could see the entire town laid out below like a child's toy. The battle, now in miniature, still swirled across Main Street. He found himself looking for Bart among the tiny figures, feeling distant and alone. A crack of thunder shook the glass and he stepped back.

Now he surveyed the room. He could see that the furniture was laid out in pockets, so groups of men could congregate. Thick armchairs and long sofas. Brass-legged tables with glass tops. Some of the tables held empty glasses and whisky bottles. A few held small mussed piles of newspapers. A large wooden desk of darkened walnut with a fine, tall-backed chair stood at the centre of a great empty space in the far corner of the room. Only one other object stood within the space, a squat black safe with a silver handle and a large combination dial in the centre. "Sterling Safe Company" was painted in gold letters on the door, and below that, "Beware: Property of Tyrus King."

Cody started to walk – and then ran – to the safe. He knelt down in front of the door and gave a quick nervous glance about to be sure he was still alone. He reached forwards and tried to turn the handle. It didn't budge. He knew it wouldn't, but he wasn't sure how else to start.

He shook his head as if to break loose an idea from his mind. He took a deep breath.

Pa used to brag sometimes that he could crack a safe. Although Cody never really believed him, he tried to remember everything that Pa had told him about safecracking now. *It's all in the ears, boy. Listen for the clicks. Then its smarts and instinct, which you ain't got. So if that don't do it, dynamite works.*

Cody reached up and set his fingers to the dial. A series of small and large ticks circled around the edge with numbers marking every tenth tick. The numbers climbed to 90, then circled back to zero. A small arrowhead on the door, close to the dial, marked the selected number. Cody leant forwards and set his ear flush against the cold steel door. A chill ran through his cheek and down the back of his neck. He could feel the blood pulsing through his veins and the nerves building in his fingertips. He thought of Bart lying on the cold, wet ground. And Map Dreamer, cold and bloody, his limp body crumpled in the mud. He took a breath.

Now Cody closed his eyes and turned the dial. He focused all his thoughts on his ears, on hearing the click. The dial rotated once, and then again. No click, only his heartbeat. He turned it again. Focused. Felt the etchings of the dial on the skin of his fingertips. Lost awareness of the closed-eye blackness in his mind. He exhaled. Turned the dial. Heard something. One click and another and another. Not the click of the combination, but the sound of the dial turning.

What did Pa tell him? *The combination clicks sound different. Louder. Deeper. If you ain't too dumb you can pick out the difference.*

But Cody couldn't pick out the difference. All the clicks sounded the same. And he could barely hear them. He pressed his ear tighter to the steel, pressed until it hurt. Tuned out the pain. Pressed his other ear closed with his thumb. Turned the dial. Click, click, click. Counted one hundred clicks. Another rotation. Another hundred clicks. All sounded the same. Or didn't. He couldn't tell one way or the other.

He pulled his head away from the door. Rubbed the sting from his ear and wiped the sweat away. Sank his face into his hands. If only he had dynamite. But he'd probably blow the map up along with the door, he knew. He was a breath away from giving up when he had an idea.

What if he could feel the clicks? As Sky Weaver taught him to feel the stone. As Sky Weaver felt the sky. As Cody himself felt the crow's feather land on his shoulder.

Cody closed his eyes again. But this time he didn't set his ear against the door. He tuned out the world all except the safe. He reached up and set his fingertips to the dial. He turned it slowly, one click at a time. Reached out with his consciousness, with his mind, with his soul. He sought the ripples, the pulses, the vibrations of sky created by each click. He listened for the pulses with his ears, on his skin, in the air he breathed.

And for an instant he heard – or felt – something. He changed the direction of the dial. His fingers rotated the numbers slowly. Again he felt a click or a pulse or a tick. Again he changed directions.

Five numbers, Pa had told him once.

Cody rotated and switched. Rotated and switched. He could feel the pulses clearly now. Or he thought he could. He could barely breathe. His fingers felt distant. The world felt distant. An energy rose inside him. He was going to open the safe. He was going to get the map. He could feel the clicks. He could feel the sky.

Cody slid his hand off the dial and moved it over the handle, where it hovered a long moment before he finally lowered his palm down onto the metal lever.

Then he closed his fingers around it and turned. But nothing happened. He opened his eyes and tried again to turn the lever. He pulled. Pushed. Put his weight into it. Slammed his fist down on the metal grip, but it didn't budge.

The energy that had risen in Cody crashed down like a lightning bolt and shocked something inside. He felt an anger rise in its place. A boiling, raging anger. Failure. He felt his muscles tense. Teeth clench. Eyes glare. He reached down and grabbed the handle of his Colt and pulled the gun from its holster. Without thinking, he raised the weapon and aimed it at the safe. His finger tensed on the trigger, but he didn't pull. He just stared at the safe, hand shaking.

He hadn't felt the pulses. He hadn't felt the sky. He hadn't felt anything.

Then he heard it. Laughter, cold and sneering. "That's quite a stand-off you got there, boy."

Cody turned to find Pa standing behind him, six-gun drawn and aimed at his chest.

Chapter 35

ONE BULLET

Cody and Pa stood square to each other, and Cody felt like it was the first time he had ever truly seen the man. Maybe this was the only way you truly could see Pa, squared off with death lurking between you. He studied his face. Hollow, sinewy cheeks. Thin, bent mouth. Sharp nose. Black eyes, dark as spent embers, and burning with hatred. Cody sometimes wondered who Pa hated most.

Now he glanced down at the Colt in his hand. The trigger felt warm and comfortable against his finger. Standing there, facing Pa, not ten paces away, all he had to do was squeeze the trigger. Whatever else might happen, the bullet would hit its mark. Cody could erase his past and his future with one finger. One bullet.

Pa shook his head and spat. "Don't think I won't put you in the ground."

Cody didn't flinch. He'd always known that was true – that Pa could kill him. He wondered now why it still bothered him. He wondered if it mattered.

A moment passed and the silence between them grew. Cody's nerves started to tingle. It wasn't like Pa to wait. *Your enemy can't kill you if he's dead,* Pa would say. Cody didn't want to give Pa the chance to strike first.

"Did you ever love Ma?" he blurted. He didn't even know where the words came from, but they stung his throat.

For a moment Pa's head turned and his eyes glanced down as if he had dropped something and was watching it fall. His cheek twitched. Then his sneer returned and he stared at Cody, unblinking. "Don't talk about yer ma," he said, almost whispered. "You didn't even know yer ma."

Cody felt his blood boil and the skin on his cheeks flush hotly. The trigger against his finger smouldered. His eyes met Pa's stare coldly. He applied the slightest pressure to the trigger. He wanted to pull it. Welcomed the moment. He hated Pa.

Now Pa forced a low laugh that chugged like a slow train. "Your filthy birth's between you and yer ma.

You can settle it soon enough."

"You're gonna kill me?"

"Don't ask stupid questions, boy."

Cody wondered if his mother had ever loved Pa. He hoped not.

Pa spat and drummed his fingers against the side of his pistol.

Cody inhaled and checked his aim, prepared to shoot – and to die. He wanted to pull the trigger, but he couldn't. His finger froze against the gun's curved steel, which suddenly felt cold against his skin. He watched Pa, waiting for him to strike, to put a bullet in his own son, and his fingers grew numb. He could barely feel the gun in his hand.

Cody wished he could visit Mrs Ryder again. He wanted to see her cradle and kiss her baby, who must have been born by now. He wanted to tell her he was sorry and hug her and feel her lips against his cheek. He wanted to hear that everything would be all right. He wasn't ready to meet his ma yet, not if it meant dying.

Then Cody heard a familiar voice.

"I don't believe I ever witnessed a more touching family reunion," bellowed Gus Grimshaw. "But if anyone shoots, I'll plug whoever's left standing."

The gunfighter stood just inside the doorway,

six-gun in each hand. Cody noticed him glance about the room and knew who he was looking for. Somewhere among the gun racks and furniture hid the assassin Morgan, his rifle aimed in their direction. The thought twisted Cody's stomach.

Grimshaw stepped forwards, his long, dark coat swaying behind him. "Come over here, son," he said, motioning with the barrel of one gun for Cody to approach. Grimshaw's eyes and his other gun never moved from Pa, who still aimed his pistol at his son.

Cody hesitated. He looked at Pa, who sneered. "Go on, boy. I don't expect no better from you."

Cody lowered his gun and shuffled towards Grimshaw.

The gunfighter laughed hoarsely. Still not looking at Cody, he said, "I see why you got no sense of humour." He shook his head. "Just stand beside me while I sort this out. Unlike your old man, I'd prefer not to kill you."

Cody raised his eyes defiantly towards the man, who still didn't return his gaze. "Maybe I'll kill you."

Grimshaw laughed.

Pa sniggered. "That boy couldn't shoot a dog."

Cody felt the defiance inside him shrivel and fall away.

Grimshaw sneered. "Shut your mouth, you mangy cur."

Pa ground his teeth and glared.

"I may let the boy shoot you when we're done." Grimshaw flashed a brief smile towards Pa, whose face stayed clenched in a stony scowl. "Don't try nuthin' foolish in the meantime."

Now Pa curled a lopsided smile and drummed his fingers on the side of his pistol. His arm moved, almost imperceptibly, in the gunfighter's direction.

"Morgan!" Grimshaw called, and a shot blasted a whisky bottle off a table not two paces from where Pa stood. The glass burst into pieces and sprayed out like blood from a wound. In Cody's mind the shards moved slowly, and he felt their vibration as they sailed through the air. Pa dropped into a half-crouch at the sound of the shot, then stood back up calmly when he saw the shattered glass fall to the floor. The shot's echo pulsed through the room and faded slowly.

"Now, Jessup," Grimshaw said, "what are you doing here?"

Pa spat. He squeezed the handle of his pistol tightly. He glared at the man.

"Answer me now, or I'll have Morgan blast off your fingers one by one. And, believe me, by the time you're down to thumbs, you'll tell me whatever I want to know."

Pa glanced accusingly at Cody then returned his glare to the gunfighter. "I come for the map."

"Of course you did." Grimshaw shook his head, grinning. The shifting of his head and the slight roll of his eyes created the opening Pa needed. He raised his arm and fired. His movement was a blur, the strike of a snake, instinctive and deadly. His gun blasted and flashed, and Grimshaw flew back through the air, arms flailing, spray of crimson in his wake, guns clattering across the floor. As his back slammed down on the hard oak, a second shot blasted – a rifle.

Cody felt the shot's echo. The pulse of sound twisted away from the barrel of Morgan's rifle and Cody perceived it as a rope he could trace back to the source. Sound and light and movement slowed in Cody's mind – Grimshaw's body bouncing off the floor, Pa's deep-set eyes opening widely, a crow's wings flapping outside the window. His senses blurred at the edges, but sharpened at the centre. He could smell each particle of gun smoke, feel each wisp float through the air. The bullet racing towards Pa spread ripples like a pebble dropped in water, and Cody could feel them collide with his skin. It all unfold so slowly. He raised his gun hand to his right, towards the rope of sound, the rifle blast, Morgan. His other hand shot forwards, fingers spread, tips stretched towards the bullet, mind stretched towards the bullet. As he squeezed the trigger of his Colt, Cody knew his bullet would strike Morgan's left thigh, which he could not see but perceived as an extension of the rope. At the same time he tracked the rippling path of the rifle's bullet. He could not see it, racing towards Pa, but sensed it clearly as if it were something that existed only in his mind. With a thought, he launched a pulse of sky towards it. The pulse did not crush, or stop, or even slow the bullet, but nicked its tail, changing its path and, rather than striking Pa's heart as Morgan intended, the deadly lead plunged into Pa's shoulder with a burst of crimson.

Time unfroze.

Pa howled and jerked away violently, dropping hard to the floor, his pistol bouncing off the leg of a nearby table.

Cody turned, arm still extended, and aimed the Colt at his father.

Pa looked down at his bloody shoulder then stared up at Cody, his expression cold and dismissive. "Ain't you gonna help me?" he said. At the same time, his hand slid slowly across the floor and hovered over the handle of his six-shooter.

Cody shook his head. "Don't pick up that gun or I'll plug you."

"Maybe you should," Pa said. His hand closed around the pistol's walnut handle. "But you won't."

Cody stared at his father. His heart beat slowly. His breath came easy. His finger felt the smooth trigger of his Colt, warm against his skin. He would shoot.

"I'm your son," he said, unblinking.

Pa's cheek twitched and his eyes slowly widened. His scowl melted to a blank, defeated expression. "I didn't love yer ma," he said. "And I sure as hell don't love you. I thought you'd be useful. But yer more trouble than yer worth."

Cody absorbed the words numbly and stared into Pa's black eyes. He wasn't sure why he had saved him from Morgan's bullet.

Pa laughed, and his hand and forearm clenched as he moved to raise his pistol. Cody squeezed the trigger of his Colt. A bullet leapt from the chamber and screeched through the barrel and out into the air. It drilled through Pa's hand and lodged itself in the handle of his gun, which tumbled from his grip and crashed through a glass tabletop.

Pa howled and grabbed his bloody hand. His breath came short and rapid and his face contorted in pain and hatred. He clenched his teeth and bits of spittle sprayed from his mouth. His eyes darted frantically and landed on Cody, boring their rage into his son. He started to move towards Cody, but held himself back, his eyes settling on the Colt pointed at his head.

"Yer gonna kill me?" he shouted savagely, mouth frothing, eyes wild, muscles taut. "Pull the trigger!"

Cody inhaled deeply. He thought of his ma and what he'd want her to see when they finally met. He wasn't sure of the answer, but he knew it wasn't a killer.

"I'm your son," he said finally. "But I'm not you."

Chapter 36

THE DEAD

Cody stepped out of the Skyscraper with the El Dorado map clutched in his fist. Upstairs, Grimshaw lay dead. Pa's bullet had drilled a hole in the gunfighter's chest and there was nothing Cody or anyone else could do to help him. Morgan had vanished. All he left behind were some empty shells and a smeared trail of blood leading to the back stairway and down. Pa sat tied in a sturdy oak chair, where Cody left him cursing and straining against the ropes. He would escape before he bled to death, but it would hurt.

With Pa out of the way, Cody had knelt once more in front of King's safe. This time, he felt each dial tick as he had felt each ripple from Morgan's bullet. The lock clicked open on his first try.

Now, Cody stepped onto the road. Light, misty rain hung in the pale, windy sky and he tipped the broad brim of his hat down over his eyes. His clothes clung to his body damply and the inside of his boots squished when he walked. He tucked the map into his pocket and touched the handle of his Colt to make sure it was still there. Then he smiled. He was alive. And he had put a bullet through Pa's gun hand and tied him to a chair. He might pay for it later, but right now it felt good. The cool air felt good.

Hooves clopped and the mustang appeared like a low grey cloud in the grey sky. Cody watched the horse trot to him and skid to a stop. He reached up and patted its neck, amazed at the animal's timing. Then he raised a boot to the stirrup and hoisted his tired body into the saddle.

"Come on, Smoke," he said. "We've got to find Bart."

The mustang whinnied and bolted down the road.

Main Street was strangely quiet. Small clusters of townsmen and shopkeepers hovered in front of open doorways and at intervals glanced up nervously from their hushed conversations. A few men shuffled along the edge of the street with heads down and hands in pockets, as if to avoid getting caught up in a gunfight that might break out at any moment. But all the gunfighters were gone or dead. Cody counted six bodies in the street. The Okwaho, too, were gone – even their dead.

Cody leapt off Smoke's back outside the hardware store where he had last seen Bart, but the old man was gone. Map Dreamer, too. Even their blood had washed away.

A middle-aged man with a thick black moustache stood inside the store with his arms wrapped to his chest. He watched Cody, squint-eyed and scowling, through the opening where the window used to be. Cody thought maybe the man recognized him and blamed him for the damage to his shop. But the man's expression eased and he unfolded an arm to point at Cody. "You were with them."

Cody nodded.

"You're looking for your friend, the white-haired man."

Cody nodded again.

"They took him. The Buffalo Riders."

Cody looked at the muddy road then back at the man. He took a shallow breath and exhaled it forcefully. "Was he dead?" The words felt wrong to Cody, even as he spoke them, and he wished he had asked if Bart was alive. But Cody knew he had asked that way because it was what he already believed.

The man looked sympathetically at Cody and wiped his mouth with the side of his hand as if he were trying to clean something away. He gave a slight shake of his head and his eyebrows rose. "Looked like it."

Cody felt the air squeezed out of his chest.

"But I don't know for certain," the man added.

"Sure," Cody mumbled. "Which way?"

The man pointed east.

Cody rode out of town and headed for Blood Hill. The rain stopped and the clouds started to part. Hazy white beams of sunlight snuck through the cracks and pointed across the sky. The air smelled dank and muddy, and Smoke's hooves made slapping sounds as they pounded the soggy road.

Cody watched the sky and thought about Gus Grimshaw. He knew the man was a hired gun, but some part of Cody believed Grimshaw would never have killed him, just as some part of Cody believed Pa would never kill him. Cody couldn't deny that he liked Grimshaw when the gunfighter wasn't being cruel. He felt sad the man was dead.

When they reached their destination, Smoke refused

to climb the hill. Cody slid down from the saddle and walked carefully between the many graves. He could see a great distance in all directions. The Scar Mountains dominated the western view. Empty, open plains extended to the north and the south, with distant grassy highlands far north. On the eastern horizon, several wagons headed west towards Fortune City. But no buffalo. No Tatanka. No Bart.

Cody stood on top of the graveyard, watching for his companions until the clouds grew puffy and white and the sky grew clear and blue. Then he saw a mule-drawn cart coming towards them, bodies piled in the back. King's men come to bury the dead. Cody scanned the horizon once more with no sign of Bart or the Tatanka. Finally, he clambered down the hill and hoisted himself into the saddle, unsure where he intended to go.

Then Cody remembered the map in his pocket. He took it out and unfolded it carefully. He studied the rivers, lakes, hills and mountain ranges, and the gold sun that marked El Dorado. He thought about the people who had died because of the map. Bart. Grimshaw. Map Dreamer. Tatanka and Okwaho. King's hired guns. Even the man at the Express outpost.

Cody's fingers clenched the edge of the map tightly,

and he thought to tear it to shreds right then and there. He felt angry at all the suffering it had caused. And at himself for having taken the map in the first place. For having wanted to find the gold. He had gone through so much for the map, and now he just wanted to be rid of it. But something in Cody wouldn't let him destroy the map. Instead, he glanced at it once more and marked the river that flowed down though the Scar Mountains and behind Fortune City. He set Smoke on a path to pick up the waterway just south of the city.

Daylight drifted away and settled into darkness as they reached the river. They stopped there and Cody unsaddled the mustang and took off his damp clothes and boots to dry them in the breeze. He leant back against a rock and watched the stars and listened to the water that moved quietly past. Smoke stood near by, chewing some tall grass that grew along the riverbank.

"I guess you knew Bart longer than I did," Cody said.

Smoke snorted.

"He saved me, you know."

Smoke chewed.

Cody watched a bright star twinkle and it reminded him of Bart's eyes. "I'm not sure what he wanted from me."

Smoke lifted his head from the grass and stepped closer to Cody, who reached out and patted the horse's neck. "I'll miss him."

The mustang nickered softly.

Cody rubbed Smoke's neck silently for a time. He wondered why the people who cared about him most seemed to die. He felt a terrible weight pressing down on his chest and he tightened his jaw. It made him angry that he felt sorry for himself but he couldn't help it. Then he started to cry and he felt angry for that too. But his anger soon vanished and all he felt was grief and loss and an emptiness where he knew there should be love. He cried and then sobbed, chest heaving, hand resting on the mustang's neck. When his tears subsided, he took a deep breath and he felt better. Not good, but better.

"You know, Smoke," he said. "I thought to tear up that map. But I don't think that would help the Tatanka. They would always think the map was out there, and always worry that it might lead someone like King or Pa to them. That's why Map Dreamer searched for it."

Chapter 37

GOING HOME

In the deep blue sky the sun appeared large as if it had plunged into a vast body of water, sending ripples of light across the world. The glare skimmed down across broad rolling hills dressed in tall, tawny grass. And a westward breeze swayed the grass and lifted larks into the sky and carried the scent of distant flowers.

Cody felt the quaking through his saddle and in the rattle of his teeth, a long thundering boom that rolled towards him as if a racing storm cloud were pouring down boulders. The grass shook like an army of thin, frightened soldiers.

Then, over the crest of the hill, the buffalo surged forwards like a river. Thousands of the dark-furred creatures pounded across the plain, humped backs churning, broad heads bent forwards. They flooded the hillside and flowed down like an unstoppable torrent. A dusty haze, flecked with hints of reflected sunlight, engulfed the herd as wave after wave of the muscled beasts rushed ahead. Cody knew that El Dorado was near.

Smoke leapt forwards and galloped towards the thundering herd, head bent low as if imagining itself one of the great beasts. The mustang dove in among them and weaved through the dusty spaces between them. Cody felt like he was careening down the rapids of a dark, swelled river. His entire body shook and the great deep booming in his ears drowned out all other sounds. They raced this way a long time, the grey mustang dancing forwards through the herd, until the land flattened and the throng slowed and Smoke drifted out of the tumult.

Ahead, the valley dipped sharply and met with a narrow stand of poplars. Behind the trees stood rows and rows of tipis. Among the dwellings, women moved about busily, working animal hides and looms. Groups of men sat in small circles, talking. And beyond the camp, a gaggle of boys played a tackling game. Cody watched them chasing and laughing. Then he heard hooves pounding deeply and two Tatanka warriors, mounted on buffalo, emerged from the trees. They rode towards Cody, slowly, spears clutched in their fists.

Cody held very still and patted Smoke's neck. The horse, too, held very still.

When the warriors reached them, they eyed Smoke strangely and exchanged words in a language Cody didn't understand. They looked at Cody and spoke to him. They pointed at Smoke and spoke more strange words.

Cody shook his head.

"I don't understand," he said. But they did not appear to understand him either.

The warriors spoke to each other once more and then spun their mounts back towards the tipis. One of the men turned towards Cody and gestured that he should follow.

○～○

A silver-haired man with a broad, weathered face emerged from the tipi. He wore a woven blanket over his shoulders and fringed buckskin trousers. Cody noticed the blanket was fastened with a small golden clip. The man looked at Cody appraisingly with deep brown eyes. Then he looked at Smoke. His eyes surveyed the horse from nose to tail. The mustang whinnied and the man nodded as if he understood.

"How did you come by this horse?" he said.

"You know my language."

"As do you." The man laughed. Then he pointed with his head towards the mustang. "How?"

"A friend," Cody said. He didn't like the interest they had taken in Smoke. He resisted the urge to touch his Colt.

The man nodded again and touched his chin as if he were thinking deeply. "I am called Buffalo Horns," he said finally.

"My name's Cody, and the horse is called Smoke."

The man pursed his lips and nodded approvingly. "Smoke."

Cody could feel eyes watching from all directions. A dozen men stood directly ahead and stared, scowling. A woman, half hidden behind a tipi, clutched a young girl and whispered in her ear, pointing. A line of boys watched him and laughed. Then one of them ran past Cody and tapped him on the arm. He howled as he raced away, and the boys watching him cheered.

Buffalo Horns looked at Cody and smiled. Then he

surveyed the onlookers and drew open the tipi's entrance. "Come," he said, gesturing towards the opening with his head. "The horse trusts you, so I trust you."

Cody glanced at Smoke then crouched down and stepped into the dwelling. A small fire burned in the middle of the room, its smoke drifting out through a gap at the tipi's pointed top. A small old woman sat on a buffalo blanket beside the fire. Her white hair was twisted into two thick braids whose ends were fastened with thin golden rings. She smiled at Cody and patted the ground for him to sit. Something in her smile reminded Cody of Mrs Ryder.

Cody and Buffalo Horns both sat.

"She is Sings Lovely," Buffalo Horns said. Cody smiled and introduced himself.

"You should eat," she said. Her voice sounded smooth and high as a bird's. She reached behind her and drew out a bowl filled with nuts and seeds and handed it to Cody. Like the clip that fastened Buffalo Horns' blanket, and the rings that secured the old woman's hair, the bowl was made of gold. Cody took the bowl in his hands and felt its heft. He was starting to understand how much gold the Tatanka must have. Every piece of jewellery. Every bowl.

He wondered what other everyday things they might

make from gold. Spoons? Knives? Arrows? Drums?

"Eat," Sings Lovely said.

Cody took a handful of nuts and tossed them into his mouth.

"Why are you here?" Buffalo Horns said. He was watching Cody's hands, which clutched the golden bowl. "What do you want?"

Cody stared down at the bowl. He could see his eyes reflected in it. "I don't want nuthin," he said. But he was thinking that if he took just one bowl, he could sell it for enough to live comfortably for a while. A dozen bowls would get him that much further. Maybe he could buy some land or start his own express business. And what did the Tatanka need with gold anyway? Wouldn't bowls of wood or clay work just as well?

Buffalo Horns cleared his throat. "Why are you here?"

Cody stared at his reflection in the gold. He inhaled and exhaled sharply. He thought about how he might hang onto the map, so he could come back from time to time. He wouldn't have to be like Pa or King; he could just take a little, just take what he needed. And there'd be plenty of gold left for the Tatanka. They wouldn't even miss it. They wouldn't even notice.

Cody reached into his pocket and grasped the map

in his fist. His knuckles brushed the gold coins he had taken from the Ryders, and his fingers began to tingle. The buzz swelled to his hands. His heartbeat quickened. The knot in his stomach uncoiled. And for the briefest instant, Cody feared Pa had snuck up behind him. He blinked and looked up from the bowl.

"I brought you something," he said finally.

The old man stared at Cody, stone-faced and silent. Sings Lovely smiled and nodded encouragingly as Cody pulled the map from his pocket and held it out to Buffalo Horns. He thought about all that Map Dreamer had given up to search for the map, and all the people who had lost their lives trying to get it. He thought about Bart.

Buffalo Horns reached out and took the map from Cody's hand, and Cody let it go.

○~○

Cody set out late that same afternoon. He didn't see how any good would come of staying with the Tatanka. And he had things to do. The *mochila* strapped to his saddle was filled with mail that he needed to drop at a Pony Express outpost. The coins jangling in his pocket needed to be returned to the Ryders along with the truth and an apology. And even though he didn't have

Bart's body, Cody wanted to mark a gravestone for the old man. He wanted to make some outwards sign that Bart had made a difference in the world. Maybe it was enough that Bart had changed Cody's life and how he lived it. Maybe, when people met Cody they would see some aspect of Bart inside of him. Even if they didn't know exactly what it was, they would recognize some quality that Cody didn't have before he met the old man. He hoped so. Still, he would mark a piece of ground for his friend.

Smoke set off at a gallop. The buffalo charged after the mustang, but the horse put a great distance between them before it even reached the top of the rise. Cody let it run until they were alone with the endless blue sky. Then he eased the grey mustang to a walk and patted its neck.

"I don't know where we are," he said, "but we need to get to the Ryders'."

Smoke whinnied, and Cody felt certain that the horse knew the way. He relaxed himself in the saddle and breathed the cool air. He soaked up the day's final rays of sunlight and listened to the clop of Smoke's hooves. He fished the pebble from his pocket and let it rest in the palm of his hand. He tried to feel its weight and to find the force to lift it skyward. He had time, he knew, to figure it out. He pursed his lips and began to whistle a tune. If the moon rose full, they would ride through the night.

ACKNOWLEDGEMENTS

There are many folks who helped me learn to tell a good story, especially my friend and teacher Terry Davis, and my friends from the creative writing program at Minnesota State University, Mankato, USA. Thank you Derek Tellier, Gordy Peuschner, Roger Hart, Tom Maltman, Jessica Gunderson, Hans Hetrick, Kristina Lilleberg, Jenny Marks, Nate LeBoutillier, Trisha Speed Shaskan, Becky Davis, Roger Sheffer and Rick Robbins. Special thanks to Nick Healy for his advice and assistance.

Thanks also to Karen and Kendal, to my family and to Jarrett for his encouragement. To Aimée Bissonette for her counsel. And to Michael Dahl and the team at Raintree for their hard work in bringing this book to the world.

MICHAEL O'HEARN

Michael O'Hearn published his first book in 2007, a graphic novel following the story of Henry Ford as he built the Model T automobile. He has since published many other books and continues to write both non-fiction and fiction. Michael lives in Connecticut, USA, with his wife, Karen, his daughter, Kendal, and her stuffed kitty, Meowy. When he's not busy writing, he likes to drum, trim bonsai trees, try yo-yo tricks and read.